MONSTER MADNESS

GUY BASS

ILLUSTRATED BY ROSS COLLINS

To my family

Scholastic Children's Books
A division of Scholastic Ltd
Euston House, 24 Eversholt Street
London, NW1 1DB, UK
Registered office: Westfield Road, Southam, Warwickshire, CV47 0RA
SCHOLASTIC and associated logos are trademarks and/or registered trademarks of Scholastic Inc.

Gormy Ruckles: Monster Boy
First published in the UK by Scholastic Ltd, 2008
Text copyright © Guy Bass, 2008
Illustrations copyright © Ross Collins, 2008

Gormy Ruckles: Monster Mischief
First published in the UK by Scholastic Ltd, 2008
Text copyright © Guy Bass, 2008
Illustrations copyright © Ross Collins, 2008

Gormy Ruckles: Monster Trouble
First published in the UK by Scholastic Ltd, 2009
Text copyright © Guy Bass, 2009
Illustrations copyright © Ross Collins, 2009

This edition published in the UK by Scholastic Ltd, 2011

Cover illustration © Ross Collins, 2011

The moral rights of the author and illustrators of this work have been asserted by them.

ISBN 978 1407 13030 9

A CIP catalogue record for this book is available from the British Library.

Printed and bound by CPI Group (UK) Ltd, Croydon, CR0 4YY
Papers used by Scholastic Children's Books are made from wood grown in sustainable forests.

1 3 5 7 9 10 8 6 4 2

www.scholastic.co.uk/zone
www.guybass.com

MONSTER BOY

Meet the Ruckles
(and try not to get eaten)

Gormy Ruckles, the monster boy, was very
small, very blue and very hairy. He had a long
tail and just one quite good fang. Gormy lived at
No. 1 Peatree Hill with his mother, Mogra the
Horrid, and his father, Grumbor the Grim. It
was the largest house on the hill, because it was
the only house on the hill.

After all, who would want to live next to
monsters?

The view from the top of the very tall tree

It was a crisp Maytober morning when Gormy
Ruckles awoke with thoughts of monstering on
his mind. After brushing his fang and combing
his fur, Gormy scampered downstairs, into the
kitchen, then out of the back door into the
garden. This all took rather a long time, as the
house was monstrously big and Gormy was very
small. He was only one-eighth-and-a-seventh

old, which was still young for a monster. However, as anyone with a passing knowledge of monsters can tell you, it is incredibly difficult to translate monster years into human years. It has something to do with sneezing and is actually quite disgusting.

Gormy ran to the end of the surprisingly charming garden, where stood the Very Tall Tree. Even compared to a full-sized monster, the Very Tall Tree was *very* tall. To Gormy it seemed *enormous*.

He dug his claws into the trunk and began

climbing, up and up until the tree grew thick with bright-green leaves, then up and up (and up and up and up!) until he reached the top.

There, perched in the tree's highest branches, was Gormy's treehouse (so-called because it was built from the bones of a Tree Monster that had once had an argument with Gormy's father).

From here Gormy could see the land beyond his home on Peatree Hill. It was the most incredible place he had ever seen, chock-full of patchwork fields, long, winding rivers and huge, distant mountains.

The treehouse was by far Gormy's favourite

place. He could happily spend hours there, trying to catch sight of a flock of sheep or a herd of cows. If he was very lucky he might even see the odd "hoomum". Hoomums were the strangest creatures Gormy had ever seen, all small and hairless and covered in bits of material (they called them "cloves"), to prevent them looking so tasty to hungry monsters!

Gormy had never once gone beyond the thick ring of trees that surrounded the house and made the top of the hill look, from the outside, just like a rather unwelcoming forest. He couldn't wait to explore the land beyond the hill! You see, Gormy Ruckles was absolutely and completely positive that he was going to be the most monstrous monster that had ever monstered in the long and glorious history of monstering. More monstrous even than his father, Grumbor, who was easily as big as a very big elephant and had so many claws, fangs and horns that by the time you had counted them all, he would have eaten you. Grumbor was one of the best, most terrifying monsters in the land, and was quite well known. After all, he went out monstering almost every week and had never once been slain.

"One day," Grumbor would tell Gormy, "you will roam the forests and the glens, roaring and growling and stamping on things. It's like riding a bike – once you learn, you never forget how to be monstrous. But for now, you must stay here on the hill, where it's safe. There'll be plenty of time for scaring and eating hoomums when you're older."

It seemed to Gormy that almost everything

fun had to wait until he was older.

Maybe I'll just stay up here in the treehouse for ever, he thought. *At least then I can see the land beyond the hill.*

He might have, too, if not for hearing his mother's familiar cry:

"Breakfast!"

2

How to be a
better Monster

Gormy rushed down (and down and down) the tree,
up the garden and into the kitchen. The giant
breakfast table was already piled high with
monstrous portions of food, everything from
pig's-neck pancakes to offal waffles to freshly
squeezed horse juice. Gormy stuffed a plateful of
kitten-on-toast into his mouth before speaking,
because it's very impolite to talk with an empty

mouth at a monster's table.

"*Please* can I visit the land beyond the hill?" he asked. It was the same question he asked every day.

"No," said his father, swallowing a mouthful of cowflakes.

"But see how monstrous I am!" said Gormy, pulling a face and baring his one quite good fang. His father only grunted. His mother, however, was much more supportive.

"Oh, Gormy, you look simply disgusting! Well done!" she said with a wide, hundred-toothed smile.

Gormy's mother was not like any mother you have ever seen. She was bright pink and so hairy that even bears were jealous of her. She didn't do too much monstering because of her weak ankles, but every now and again she would sneak out and terrify passers-by or ransack the odd village. How she loved to ransack!

"You keep it up, my little furball!" his mother continued. "When you're ready, you'll monster with the best of them."

"But I'm ready now!" pleaded Gormy.

"I said *no*," said Grumbor, in a voice that sounded like a hundred rocks being smashed together. "No going anywhere until you're a *real* monster. Remember what happened to Old Uncle Gobog?"

Actually, Gormy didn't really remember much at all about Old Uncle Gobog. He remembered that he was big and jolly and purple, and that he had gone out monstering one day and had never come back. But he knew that when his father said "Remember what happened to Old Uncle Gobog", all talk of leaving the hill should stop. Gormy sighed.

"Finish your kitten," said Grumbor, getting down from the table with a ground-shaking thud. "It's time for your lesson."

Gormy knew in his heart of hearts (he had two) that his father wanted to make him the best monster he could be, because no one cared as much about monstering as Grumbor. The only thing he took half as seriously was the crossword in the weekly *Monster Gazette*, which contained no clues and was made up entirely of monstrous noises such as "Greeeeeeep!" and "Slowb-slowb!" It was the hardest crossword ever invented, and Gormy's father loved it. But monstering was his true passion.

Gormy fetched his **How to be a Better Monster** book from his room and made his way to the study for his five-hundred-and-fivety-fifth lesson in how to be a better monster.

"Dad?" said Gormy, looking around. He couldn't see him anywhere (and his father was quite hard to miss). He scrambled up the chair leg until he reached the seat, then laid the book on his desk and began flicking lazily through the pages. Inside were recorded all five-hundred-and-fivety-four of Gormy's lessons, with illustrations. His favourites, in reverse order of monstrousness, were:

Lesson 42 – The Key to Monstering is Timing.

This lesson involved a number of monstrous games, including *Smash! Thing!* (a classic monster game in which things were smashed).

In another game, *The Eat Feat*, the player had to study a selection of fruits and decide which piece was ready to be scared into ripeness. Gormy was very good at this game.

Then:

Lesson 63 and a half – The Key to Monstering is Location.

This included nine rounds of *Scare Me Here, Scare Me There*, which was sort of like hide-and-seek with added scariness, and was very difficult to play when you were a giant monster. The lesson also included Gormy's all-time favourite game, *Excuse Me, Is That Your Monster?*, which had to be seen to be understood.

And finally:

Lesson 2 – The Key to Monstering is a Perfect Roar.

This lesson, as you might imagine, was all about roaring. Now, having a perfect roar wasn't as simple as just roaring perfectly. A monster had to master anywhere between four and fourteen-hundred individual monster sounds before being able to attempt a proper roar. These included:

GrRraiiaEeghh!
BRRrOWWghg!
GrrOOogH!
YaAAiaghh!

... and of course the ever-popular

GRrRRAAaaAGGH!

After his first few dozen lessons, Gormy realized there really was a lot to monstering. It made him even more excited about exploring the land beyond the hill.

Gormy stared out of the study window, and began to daydream as usual. But, for the first time in his life, something rather odd happened. His daydream slowly became a bit of an idea, which in turn became the beginning of sort of a plan. It was such an excellent sort of a *plan* that Gormy had to try hard not to giggle in expectation.

It was a plan to *escape*.

3

Lesson five-hundred-and-fivety-five

Gormy realized his plan to visit the land beyond the hill would need to be monstrously clever. He would need equipment and supplies to keep him going on his adventure. He would have to get past his parents on the way out, and get back before they noticed he'd gone. The problem was, Gormy's mother and father always liked to know where he was.

Thoughts of his father shook Gormy back to reality. Where *was* he? He definitely wasn't in the study. Had he forgotten about the lesson? That seemed very unusual. He'd never been late for a lesson before.

Gormy decided to look for him. He picked up his book, but as he did so a piece of paper fell out and on to the floor. Gormy unwrapped it carefully, until it was many times larger than he was. Upon the paper was written:

SCARE ME
(I'LL BE IN THE
GARDEN)
Love, DAd

His father had set him a challenge! Gormy ran into the kitchen, from where he could see the back garden. There, as promised, was his father, sitting in a chair with his back to the house. It was a big chair covered in a large blanket, so all Gormy could see was the top of his father's head.

Of course, Gormy's father knew Gormy was coming, but Gormy was confident. If he was quiet enough, if he used his father's teachings and mastered his stalk, skulk and pounce, he could still creep up silently and be hyper-terrifying.

Gormy crawled on his paws and knees from the back door, down the path, and across the lawn. He crawled up behind the chair and took a deep, noiseless breath into all four of his lungs. This would be the roar to end all roars. It would shake the walls of the house and echo into the valley below. Birds would scatter from their perches in high trees, and sheep would bleat their "It's-the-end-of-the-world!" bleat.

Gormy held his breath, and dug his claws into the ground. He was just about to let rip when, from behind him:

GRrRRAAaaAGGH!

It was the most terrifying noise Gormy had

ever heard! He screamed in horror and ran down the garden, twice as fast as he had ever run before. He clambered up the Very Tall Tree as fast as his hairy blue legs could carry him. He reached his treehouse and waited, shivering, for what seemed like an eternity. Then he heard another noise.

It was the sound of footsteps, each one as loud as thunder. They shook the leaves of the Very Tall Tree as they moved closer and closer. Within moments, the roaring who-knows-what was at the foot of the tree.

"M – Mummy. . ." he whimpered from the treehouse.

"Not Mummy," came the reply. "It's your father."

Gormy peered out from the treehouse.

Sure enough, far below, there stood his father, complete with a huge bald spot on his head, and in his hands a clump of his hair and two of his horns.

"The key to monstering," said his father "is to expect the unexpected." Then he wandered back in the house, whistling an un-monstrous tune.

He cut off his hair and his horns and put them on top of the chair! thought Gormy. *To make it look as if he was sitting there! All to teach me a lesson!*

Gormy had to admit, his father was *very* good

at being a monster. (He also decided, secretly, that he was a bit weird.) Gormy longed to be even half as monstrous. Even half-a-quarter!

But as long as he was stuck on Peatree Hill, he would never know what it was like to be a *real* monster. All Gormy needed was a chance to prove himself! A chance to show everyone how pant-wettingly terrifying he really was. Now, more than ever, Gormy knew that he had to go to the world beyond the hill.

It was time to put his plan into action.

Gormy the Hideous

Gormy made his way to his room and began emptying his Big Chest of Monstrously Excellent Things on to the floor.

"What's all this, then?" came a tiny, gruff voice.

"Mike!" said Gormy, as a green, greasy-looking insect crawled through his window.

Mike was a scuttybug, not much bigger than a

beetle perched on the back of another seven beetles. He was Gormy's only friend. Monsters can't eat scuttybugs (it makes their tongues sting) so Mike was never nervous in the company of Gormy's family. He also loved to visit because scuttybugs eat a lot of dung, and consider monster dung to be the softest, tastiest dung of all.

"I've got a plan, Mike," said Gormy, lining up an array of strange-looking objects on the floor, "and it's a very secret plan, so you can't tell *anyone*."

"If there's one thing a scuttybug's good at, it's secret-keeping," said Mike. "That, and rolling dung into a ball. So, what's the plan?"

"I'm going to the land beyond the hill," whispered Gormy.

"*THE LAND BEYOND THE HILL?*" yelled Mike, his buggy eyes even buggier than normal.

"ShhHHhhh!" said Gormy. "Secret!"

"Say no more," said Mike, before pointing a slimy green leg at the objects on the floor. "What's all this, then?"

"This is everything I'm taking on my very secret adventure," said Gormy. "I need to see if it'll fit in my backpack."

Lined up on the floor was:

🌸 **ONE APPLE**

(in case Gormy got hungry)

🌸 **ONE LARGE WORM**

(to take away the taste of the apple)

🌸 **TWO SOAP SWEETS**

(to keep Gormy's teeth clean and monstrous)

🌸 **ONE SING-A-LONG STONE**

(in case the outside world was too quiet)

🌸 **ONE B.O.S. or BOX OF SURPRISES**

(in case Gormy himself wasn't surprising enough)

● ONE NEVER-ENDING NOTEBOOK
(in which to record the more exciting
aspects of Gormy's adventure)
● ONE PENCIL
(in order to make writing in the notebook easier.
Gormy, being a monster boy, wasn't a big fan of
pencils and generally preferred to use a mouse
with its head bitten off, but he hadn't managed
to catch one)

"You'd better leave room for *me* in that
backpack," said Mike. "I can show you all
the sights: the really big pile of cow dung, the
not-quite-fallen-down tree, the patch of
yellowy grass—"

"And hoomums?" said Gormy, beaming.

"Oh yes, tons of hoomums," said Mike.

"If you like that sort of thing."

"How many are there?" asked Gormy, wide-eyed.

"More than I can count on my six legs," replied Mike.

"Millions!" cried Gormy excitedly. "Think how much scaring I could do!"

"Oh yeah," said Mike. "There'd be a lot of scaring going on that day, the day Gormy the Hideous stomped into town."

"*Gormy the Hideous*," whispered Gormy, almost afraid of his own name.

"How are you planning on getting out of the house, then?" asked Mike. "Won't your mum and dad notice you're missing?"

"That's the bit I haven't sorted out yet," said Gormy. "They always want to know where I am and what I'm doing."

As if on cue, Gormy heard the sound of footsteps tramping up the stairs. He frantically scooped everything off the floor and into the chest (including Mike, though he didn't really mean to). He had just managed to close the lid and sit on the chest when his mother came into his bedroom.

"Come on, puffball, it's time for your chores," she said.

"Great, chores!" said Gormy, eager to get his mother out of the room. He leapt off the chest, grabbed his mother by the ankle-hair and dragged her downstairs. He failed to hear the faint cry coming from inside the chest.

"Oi! I'm still in here . . . Hello? Hello?"

Gormy's sheep

Gormy's mother had laid out six huge saucepans for him to polish on the kitchen table. Gormy picked up a monster-sized cloth and set to work, cheerfully daydreaming of the land beyond the hill. His mother kept a watchful eye, making sure he polished all those hard-to-reach places (and for a monster boy, almost all places are hard to reach).

Gormy's mother was particularly clean and tidy, which is rare for a monster. For example, The Glum of Blackstead Heath prides himself on being dirty. He is so filthy and disgusting that his armpits grow mould.

He won first prize in every category related to poor personal hygiene at the last Annual Rural and Suburban Monster and Beast Awards.

Then there's Lom the Foul (who smells like a million rotten eggs), The Knobbly Gob (who has never *once* had a wash), and of course any of the various breeds of Spew Goblin, but the less said about them the better.

Gormy, like most monster boys, wasn't too bothered about keeping clean, and certainly wasn't a fan of housework, except for polishing. When Gormy polished silverware, it gleamed like nothing you have ever seen. As monsters don't usually have mirrors (in case their own reflection terrifies them), this was Gormy's only real opportunity to see how scary he could look.

Gormy stared at his distorted reflection in the huge, gleaming saucepan. He made a very scary face, hoping he might terrify himself.

"Wouldn't you rather practise on something real?" said his father, coming in from the garden. He had one of his huge hands behind his back.

"What do you mean?" asked Gormy.

"Come into the garden," said Gormy's father. "I've brought you something."

Gormy dashed out of the back door into the garden. There, by the garden shed, was what looked like . . . *a cage*! It was small and square and built from wooden planks. For a terrible moment Gormy wondered if it was his new bedroom.

"What's it for?" he asked, nervously. It was then that he heard a strange squeak. No, wait, not a squeak; a *bleat*.

"This is what I brought you," said Grumbor, bringing his hand out from behind his back. There, gripped gently between his claws, was a real, live sheep.

"Is that for me?" squealed Gormy.

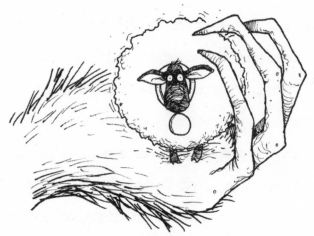

"I've decided that it's time you put your monstering lessons into practice," said Grumbor.

Gormy stared at the sheep. The sheep stared back. He had never seen a sheep close up. It was like a smelly, dirty cloud with legs.

"What do I do with it?" asked Gormy.

"You will *scare* it," replied Grumbor. "A sheep is the easiest of all animals to scare because it's stupid. When you have scared the sheep, I will bring you another animal to scare. Then another, and another, until you have learned to scare everything. Then you will be scarier than any animal."

Gormy remembered from his monstering lessons that the scariest animal of all was a wolf. There are four important things to remember about wolves:

- Wolves look like big wild dogs and hate everything but other wolves
- Wolves eat sheep, goats and anything smaller than a very big cow
- Wolves are usually called names like Cecil and Percy
- Wolves are the scariest of all animals

"Will I be scarier than a wolf?" asked Gormy.

"A wolf?" snorted Grumbor. "A wolf is nothing. You will be a *monster*."

"I'll scare that sheep so much its cloud will fall off!" Gormy beamed, more excited than ever about his monstrous potential.

"You'll keep him here, in this pen," said Grumbor. "You'll graze him in the garden. Until the day you scare this sheep, it is yours to look after." He pointed his huge finger at a collar around the sheep's neck. Upon it was a small gold badge that said: Gormy's Sheep. "Do you understand?" he added.

"I . . . I suppose," said Gormy. He wasn't sure whether he'd been given a present or a chore.

"I expect you to keep it safe and healthy," said Grumbor, adding, with a monstrous half-smile, "and, if you can manage it, absolutely terrified."

And with that, Grumbor tramped back into the house, leaving Gormy alone with the sheep. Gormy knew something important had just happened. His father expected something of him. He took a deep breath and roared a very scary roar:

GReeOAArrgghh!

The sheep did not look at all frightened. Gormy tried again:

GReEoOAArgghH!

The sheep blinked, but not in a particularly scared way. Gormy tried a third and a fourth roar, but still nothing. The sheep just stood there, staring back at him. Perhaps it simply didn't understand how scary Gormy was. Sheep were stupid, after all. Gormy kicked the cage in frustration, just as his mother came into the garden.

"Oh, Gormy, don't worry," she said knowingly. "These things take time – don't feel you have to rush it." She stroked him on the head with a giant pink finger. "You'll be a proper monster before you know it. Oh, and speaking of monstering, don't forget that tonight is your father's *Big Night Out*."

"Big . . . *Night*. . ." began Gormy, a million thoughts suddenly flooding his monster-boy brain. He could barely contain an excited yelp. His mother was right; he had forgotten all about the Big Night Out!

This was it, the final part of the plan!

The Big Night Out

A Big Night Out occurred once every full moon. This was the night when Gormy's father would monster twice as hard as normal. He would scare and tear and frenzy and ravage with such force that the whole valley would quake.

"The key to monstering," he would say, "is keeping the hoomums on their toes."

A Big Night Out was always followed by a

Surprisingly Long Nap, which lasted one day and one night. The whole family would join in. After the nap everyone would enjoy a mouth-watering feast of stuffed pony (the pony having been stuffed with a pig, a goat and a chicken), but it was the Surprisingly Long Nap that was so important to Gormy's plan. A day and a night was more than enough time for him to have an adventure.

After waving off his father, Gormy rushed upstairs to his bedroom and his Big Chest of Monstrously Excellent Things. As he opened it, Mike scrambled out, gasping for air.

"Ca ... can't ... b ... br ... *breathe*!" he wheezed.

"Great news!" cried Gormy, far too excited to notice Mike's distress. "This is it! The Big Night Out is happening and we can go and they'll be asleep which I always forget but then Mum told me and—"

"Whoa, horsey!" said Mike. "What are you on about?"

Gormy took a deep breath, and explained all about the Big Night Out and the Surprisingly Long Nap.

"All we have to do is wait until morning," he concluded. "It's what we've been waiting for!"

"You'll have time to scare every living thing in the valley!" said Mike.

Gormy stared out of the window as night

began to fall over Peatree Hill. A grin spread slowly across his face.

"I'll be a real monster. . ."

7

The land beyond the hill

It seemed to take for ever for Grumbor to return from his Big Night Out, and it was all Gormy and Mike could do to stay awake.

They waited in Gormy's bedroom for what seemed like the whole of cow-eating season (monsters tended to eat animals according to seasons to give the hoomums a chance to breed more. Except for goats. Goats were evil and therefore fair game all year round). But sure enough, as dawn broke over the hill, Gormy heard the familiar crunch and creak of the front door.

Gormy and Mike waited behind the bedroom door for precisely five minutes and five seconds before his father's loud snoring indicated the coast was clear.

"Come on, Mike," whispered Gormy as he peeked round the bedroom door. "It's time."

Mike climbed into Gormy's backpack and they made their way silently down the landing and past the door to his parents' bedroom. Gormy hopped down the monstrously large stairs, through the kitchen and out of the back door. In front of him stretched the long back garden, the Very Tall Tree, and beyond. The dense ring of trees was all that stood between Gormy's world and a world of monstrous adventure.

"Are we there yet?" came the voice from inside the backpack.

"Shhh!" said Gormy, setting off at a slow creep down the garden. As he passed the sheep-pen he whispered, "See you when I'm a *real* monster, sheep."

Then he stopped dead in his tracks.

His head turned slowly towards the cage. He blinked hard to make sure he was seeing what he was seeing. The door was open! It creaked slightly as it blew back and forth in the breeze.

The sheep was gone!

"Are we there yet?" said Mike again, poking his greasy green head out of the backpack.

"My sheep. . ." muttered Gormy, his voice shaking with terror. "My sheep's not there! I must have left the pen door open!"

"Oh well," said Mike merrily. "Easy come, easy go."

"You don't understand. . ." said Gormy. "My dad's going to *kill* me."

"Eh?" began Mike, as Gormy sped on all fours down the garden, desperate to catch a whiff of the sheep's funny smell.

"Whoa, horsey!" cried Mike from the backpack. "What's the rush?"

"I can smell him!" said Gormy, scampering as fast as he could, past the Very Tall Tree and onwards, until—

Gormy stopped. Before him was the thick wall of trees. It was dark and gnarled and twisted. And there was something else: a tiny shred of wool, caught on a tree branch like a trapped cloud.

"He's gone through. . ." whispered Gormy. "He's gone through the trees to the land beyond the hill."

"Now look," began Mike, "why don't we stop for a well-earned dung-rolling break and then—"

But it was too late. Gormy had clambered into the wall of trees! They were so thick and tightly woven that it was almost completely dark. Gormy found it hard to tell where he was. Had he not been so worried about what his father would do to him, he might have found it all rather spooky.

The further Gormy climbed, the more dense and tangled the trees became. Soon he had lost all sense of direction, forward or backwards, down or up! Then, finally, he saw a shaft of light in front of him.

Gormy used his tail to wrap around a nearby branch. He swung around the branch twice to get up a good speed, then let go! He crashed through the branches and out the other side, landing with a definite FUD!

Gormy shook his head and brushed leaves, twigs and foresty mess from his fur. He looked up.

He was in the land beyond the hill.

Gormy had never been anywhere that was not surrounded by walls, even in his treehouse. As he stared, open-mouthed, at the steep hill stretching out below him, he suddenly felt smaller than ever. His brain was filled with possibilities.

This land was wild and cold and untidy and went on for ever. Thick, sweet smells filled Gormy's nose, grass smells and flower smells and smells he didn't even recognize. The colours seemed to jump into his eyes and bounce around, and everywhere he turned there was something new to see. Beyond the hill were cliffs, rivers, fields . . . in the far distance he could even see what looked like a hoomum village.

"Well?" said Mike, poking out of the backpack. "What d'you think?"

"*There's so much of it. . .*" whispered Gormy with delight.

"You bet!" said Mike. "See that rock over there? That's my favourite sunbathing rock. And that bit of damp grass over there is—"

"Wait. . ." said Gormy, his ears pricking up. What was that noise? He knew he recognized it. His pointy blue ears twitched as he listened.

There it was again! It was like a strange squeak. No, wait, not a squeak – a *bleat*. Then another, and another, and another.

"Sheep!" cried Gormy.

Gormy picked himself up and scampered down the hill towards the bleating. Sure enough, grazing under a little tree was not one, not four, but a whole flock of sheep!

Gormy slowed to a skulk in the long grass, and

edged ever closer until he was in proper monstering distance. And there, in the middle of the white, woolly mass, he saw it.

"There! That's my sheep!" he whispered.

"How can you tell it's yours?" said Mike. "They all look the same to me."

"I'd know my sheep anywhere," said Gormy. "And anyway, it has a collar with 'Gormy's Sheep' on it."

Gormy crawled on his belly through the long grass as quietly as he could, careful not to scare the sheep into running off (he naturally assumed that just because *his* sheep was too stupid to be scared, that didn't mean they all were).

Suddenly, Gormy noticed something out of the corner of his eye. It was a large, dark shape, like a shadow, moving through the grass. He tried to get a better look, when he heard a rustling sound to his right. There was another one! This one was closer, and Gormy could see it was covered in grey fur.

What *was* it?

They definitely seemed to be heading for the flock. Gormy poked his head up to get a better look. As he did so, he heard a sound behind him. He looked back. Something leapt towards him! Gormy ducked and the huge shadowy creature jumped right over him. This time, Gormy got a good look.

"That thing almost had our heads off!" said Mike, poking out of the backpack. "Did you see what it was?"

Gormy's eyes grew wide.

"A wolf!"

Full of Surpises

Gormy got to his feet. He saw the three wolves break into a run towards the flock. The sheep panicked, and scattered in all directions.

"Good, eh?" said Mike, over the sound of terrified bleating. "Bet you didn't think you'd see real, live wolves. Let's hang about, see how many sheep they pick off."

The wolves divided the flock. With backs

hunched and teeth bared, they waited for the time to strike. They were much bigger than Gormy had imagined, twice as big as he was and surprisingly fierce-looking. He was quite glad that he didn't have to go anywhere near them.

"They're almost like . . . monsters," said Gormy in admiration. He watched the wolves encircle one of the smallest sheep. It was frozen to the spot with fear. The wolves paced slowly around it, snarling and biting the air.

Gormy got quite excited about the monstrously horrid things that might happen next. He couldn't look away.

It was just then that he noticed something slightly different about the sheep. It had something around its neck . . . a collar!

"That's my sheep!" shouted Gormy. "They're going to eat my sheep!"

"Blimey," said Mike. "That's a bit of bad luck."

Without thinking, Gormy rushed down the hill towards the wolves.

"Stop, you . . . you *wolves*!" he cried. "That sheep's not for eating!"

It's safe to say that Gormy didn't really have a plan at this point. He rushed at the wolves, waving his arms about and shouting things like "Get your own!" and "Put those fangs away!" By the time Gormy reached them, the wolves had turned away from the sheep and fixed their gaze on *him*.

The largest of them gnashed its teeth, its ears flat against its head. Gormy skidded to a halt. The wolf growled and tensed its shoulders as if to pounce.

"This could end in tears," said Mike.

It was at this moment that Gormy did a very un-monstrous thing. He ran away as quickly he could.

"Faster please, Gormy!" said Mike as he looked back. Unfortunately, wolves are much faster than monster boys. Within seconds, the largest wolf pounced. Gormy's face was pushed into the ground, giving him a mouthful of grass

and mud. Gormy tried to shout "Get off!" but
it sounded more like "Gmf mmff!" It certainly
didn't stop the wolf opening its jaws to bite.

Mike scuttied inside Gormy's backpack as
the wolf lunged. Its teeth sank into the soft
material and it shook its head from side to side.
Gormy, still attached to the backpack, was
lifted into the air!

"*AAAaaAAhHH!*" he screamed, as the wolf

shook him in its jaws. Finally the backpack ripped, and Gormy was flung through the air! The contents of the backpack (including Mike) were strewn across the hill.

"Mike!" cried Gormy. "Are you all right?"

But there was no answer. Gormy got to his feet. The wolves were already after him again. Saliva dripped from their mouths as they closed in. Gormy took a step back.

TONK!

He'd knocked into something! He looked down and saw a small red box.

"The B.O.S.!" he cried.

Now the thing with a Box of Surprises is you never know what you're going to get, and each box is good for only one surprise. Still, as he was about to be wolf-meat, Gormy thought he would take a chance. He opened the box:

BOOOOOOOOOM!

Fireworks! They shot out of the box and exploded all around, lighting up the whole sky! And not just one or two – there was every firework you could imagine! Whirly Geezers, Spinaroos, Flap-a-Ting Whizz-Bangs, Mucky Melons, String-Bean-Bam-Bombs, Flinging Millies, even a Bluster-Buster! All around him, explosions of colour and noise filled the air! *BANG!* after *BOOM!* after *WheeeEEE* after Fooosh!

Needless to say, the wolves turned tail and ran.

"It's about time our luck improved," came a tiny, gruff voice from nearby.

"Mike!" said Gormy. "You're OK!"

"Takes more than a shake to rattle a scuttybug," said Mike with a wink. "I tell you what, that's a crackingly good Box of Surprises."

"Come on!" said Gormy, scooping Mike into his hand. "You too, sheep!" he added. But his sheep was still frozen to the spot with fear, and by now the explosions had all but died down. Gormy could see the wolves in the distance, getting ready to attack again. There was nothing else for it. He grabbed the sheep by its two back legs, flung it on his back, and *ran*.

"They're coming back!" said Mike. Sure enough, the wolves were giving chase once more. Gormy looked up the hill to the ring of trees in the distance.

"Nearly there!" he said, running as fast as his little blue legs could carry him. The trees were almost close enough to touch.

"Keep going!" said Mike. "But whatever you do, don't look back."

Of course, this made Gormy look back. He was met by the snarling, drooling head of a wolf!

Gormy panicked and tripped, toppling head over heels. Mike and the sheep landed roughly on the edge of the tree line.

Gormy tried to get up, but the largest wolf was upon him again. Its paw was on his chest, pinning him down. Saliva dripped on to Gormy's face.

Gormy drew a long, fearful breath into his lungs as the wolf opened its jaws. . .

GREEOOAARGGH!

That was no wolf! Gormy Ruckles had found his roar! True, it wasn't all that spectacular, but it was monstrous enough to make the wolf take a step back.

Gormy didn't wait to see if he could do better. He grabbed Mike and his terrified sheep and dived into the wood, running and leaping as only a truly monstrous monster boy can.

"Top-notch roar!" said Mike. "Today's just full of surprises, isn't it?"

Once Gormy had cleared the trees, he ran all the way up the garden until he reached the sheep cage. He put the sheep inside and locked the door.

"Did it. . ." he said, collapsing on to the ground. He was covered in twigs and leaves and wolf-spit, but he was happy. Nothing else could go wrong. Everything was going to be fine.

It was then that he heard his mother's voice.

"Gormy Ruckles, what are you doing out of bed?"

9

The smell of a monstrous breakfast

Gormy looked back at the house. His mother
and father were coming out of the back door.
He had been found out.

"I . . . I . . ." began Gormy, desperate to think
of a clever excuse or two. He looked to Mike for
help, but the scuttybug had scuttied off.

"Did you hear the fireworks too?" continued
his mother. "We heard them from our bedroom

and came out to get a closer look."

"Looks like we missed it," added Grumbor, yawning.

"Must be the hoomums," said Mogra, shrugging. "They can be very peculiar sometimes."

"Must be," said Gormy, breathing a secret sigh of relief.

"And what's *this*?!" bellowed Grumbor, pointing to the sheep-pen.

"Oh, Gormy, look what you've done!" cried Mogra.

Gormy panicked. What had they seen? What had he forgotten?

"I'm so *proud* of you!" continued Mogra. "You scared your sheep!"

Gormy looked at his sheep.

It *was* completely terrified!

"You've scared something!"
said Grumbor, patting
Gormy on the head with a
finger. "You've taken your
first steps to becoming a real
monster."

Gormy thought it best not to say anything.
He just looked up at his father with a wide grin.

"Well, since we're all up," said Mogra, "why
don't we have ourselves a celebration breakfast
before bedtime?"

Before long, the smell of a monstrous
breakfast wafted through the house on Peatree
Hill. Gormy didn't even wait for his mother to
call before taking his seat at the breakfast table.

"You must tell us how you scared your

sheep," said Mogra, spooning out a monstrous portion of freshly made porridge into his tiny bowl. "Was it very difficult?"

"More difficult than I thought it would be," said Gormy, as the deliciously meaty smell wafted up his nose (monstrous porridge is of course made entirely from mashed meat). He took a huge, tasty mouthful, then, without pausing to chew, he took another.

CLUNK!

Gormy had bitten into something hard. He reached into his mouth and fished out a gold badge. Upon it was an inscription: Gormy's Sheep. He stared at his mother, his jaw open.

"Nothing like terrified sheep for breakfast!"

said his mother with a cheerful wink. "The fear really brings out the flavour, don't you think?"

Lesson five hundred and fivety-six: The key to monstering

After breakfast (which he didn't finish), Gormy went back to his bedroom. By now, he was very much in need of a Surprisingly Long Nap. He was about to get into bed when he spotted his **How to be a Better Monster** book. He turned to the first blank page.

"Lesson five hundred and fivety-*six*," Gormy said to himself. "The key to monstering . . . is *getting away with it.*"

Gormy reached for his pencil to write it down, but he'd lost it somewhere in the land beyond the hill. Then he remembered that, anyway, writing with a pencil is *very* un-monstrous.

So he found the first mouse he could, and bit off its head.

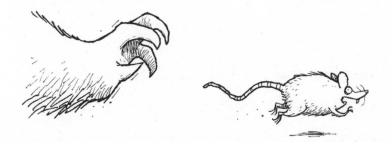

MONSTER MISCHIEF

How to Throw Rocks and Influence People

Gormy sat at the breakfast table, eating his bowl of hamsters so quickly that he started to cough up hairballs.

"Gormy Ruckles, what have I told you about chewing your food? Do you want to give yourself gut-ache?" asked Gormy's mother.

Gormy decided it was one of those questions he didn't really have to answer. Why would anyone *want* to give themselves gut-ache? Apart from the Witch of Goggan Moor, who only ate angry wasps.

"Can I get down from the table?" asked Gormy, although with his mouth full it sounded like, "Cud I geddum bubba day-bull?". Gormy's mother understood him perfectly. After all, it's rude *not* to talk with your mouth full at a monster's table.

"You *may* not go anywhere until you've finished your breakfast," she said. Gormy's mother was a large, pink monster, and was at least forty-eight times more monstrous than any mother you've ever met. She was as big as two hippos glued together and had more hair than all three finalists in last year's Hideously Hairy Monster contest.

Who cares about breakfast on a day like this? thought Gormy. Today was more monstrously exciting than the first Monstrously Exciting Day – the day when the first monster, Mon the Monstrous, scared his first woolly mammoth!

Today was ROCK THROWING DAY!

Gormy had never had a lesson in throwing before. The ability to throw a really big rock (or tree or horse or cow) was the measure of a truly monstrous monster. As Gormy's father, Grumbor, always said, "A hoomum will be twice as scared of a monster who can throw than one who can't."

Grumbor was especially good at throwing things. He had won the silver medal at the

Monster's Third National Throwing, Hurling
and Lobbing tournament, and had twice broken
the world record for long-distance Sheep
Tossing.

Gormy had already written the lesson number
in his **How to be a Better Monster** book. He
opened the book and stared gleefully at the
page.

"*Please* may I please get down from the
table?" he begged, before swallowing the last of
his hamsters.

Gormy's mother looked at him sternly.

"Where are your manners today, Gormy?" she asked.

"Oh sorry, Mum," said Gormy, then let out an almighty

BUUURRRP!

"That's better," said Gormy's mother. "Now run along."

Do Not Throw

Gormy scampered out of the kitchen door as fast as his hairy, blue legs could carry him. He had made it halfway down the garden when he heard a tiny, gruff voice.

"Where are you off to then?"

"Mike!" said Gormy.

Perched on a monster-sized plant pot was his only real friend, Mike the Scuttybug. Mike looked how a beetle would look in a nightmare about ugly, monstrous beetles. He was greasy, green and smelled faintly of his favourite food – poo.

"Thinking of doing a spot of throwing, are we?" Mike asked. "I've been watching your dad lobbing rocks all morning."

"I'm going to be the best thrower ever! Hop on, quick," said Gormy, offering Mike a furry, blue paw.

Mike scuttied on to Gormy's arm and they made their way to the bottom of the garden. It wasn't long before they spotted Gormy's father.

Grumbor Ruckles was a huge, dark blue monster, with tusks as big as branches. He had more monstrousness per square inch than any other monster in the valley. He was standing by the thick wall of trees that surrounded the house, and throwing large rocks right over it.

"Dad!" cried Gormy excitedly. Grumbor turned just as he was about to throw. The rock flew out of his hand towards Gormy.

"Eek!"

squeaked Gormy and Mike together, before jumping out of the way of the boulder.

It whooshed past Gormy's head and crashed on to the lawn.

"You know better than to sneak up on a monster when he's throwing things," grumbled Grumbor as he lumbered towards Gormy. "The key to monstering is keeping your head while all about you are having theirs knocked off. Are you all right?"

"Yeah, great!" said Gormy. Now he was even *more* excited about his lesson. Having things thrown at you was nearly as monstrous as throwing them! He stared at the rock next to him. "Can I throw it? Can I?" he asked.

"Let's start with something a little smaller," said Grumbor, before loping back down the garden. Gormy and Mike followed him to a huge pile of rocks of various sizes and shapes. There must have been a hundred of them! Maybe even a hundred and two! (Monsters can count piles of things very quickly.) Grumbor searched through the rocks until. . .

"A-ha! This one should do for starters. Hold out your hand."

Gormy's father didn't seem to be holding anything at all. He just had his finger and thumb pressed carefully together. He reached over to Gormy, and opened his fingers. The smallest rock in the world plopped into Gormy's hand.

"It's tiny. . ." said Gormy. "Can't I throw something bigger?"

"Don't try to stomp before you can walk," said Grumbor. "Now then, let's see you throw that rock over the trees."

Gormy looked down at the pebble his father

had given him, and
shrugged. He reached
his arm all the way
back, and threw!

plud

The rock landed at the edge of the trees, only
a few paces from where Gormy and his father
were standing.

"Nice try," said Mike, sort of encouragingly.

"Still too big, need something smaller,"

Grumbor mumbled to himself. Of course, as a monster, even his quietest mumble was really quite easy to hear. Gormy's pointy blue ears drooped with disappointment as Grumbor pulled out an even tinier pebble from the pile.

"Try imagining you're aiming at something," said Grumbor. "Pretend that on the other side of those trees is a herd of really evil goats. Or a big hoomum village! Yes, pretend that when you throw your rock, it lands on a nice, new hoomum house."

Gormy imagined a lovely hoomum house, built out of the finest wood and thatch. He imagined several hoomums standing next to it and saying things like "This is the nicest house we've ever built!" and "I do hope nothing bad happens to it!"

"SMASH!" said Gormy with glee. He gripped the rock tightly between his paws and threw the rock as hard as he could.

CLUD

It bounced off the trunk of a tree and rolled back into the garden. Gormy deflated like a balloon. He looked up at his father, but Grumbor simply shook his head a little.

"Not ready. . ." he mumbled.

"I am ready, I am!" cried Gormy in desperation. "I can throw the biggest rock in the garden! I can. . ."

It was then Gormy spotted it.

A large, grey rock, set apart from the pile. It was unremarkable except for one thing. Carved into the face of the rock were three words:

"What about that one?" said Gormy.

Gormy's father laughed so loudly that all the birds in the trees flew off in fright, and kept flying until they were quite lost and had to make new homes in new trees far, far away.

"That rock's for monsters, not monster *boys*," said Grumbor. "That's the DO NOT THROW rock. It's the most *unthrowable* rock in world. For centuries, monsters came to Peatree Hill to try and throw this rock. It was the greatest challenge any monster could face. One after the other they came, so that they might be declared Most Monstrous Monster (Probably in the World) Ever. Many monsters have tried to throw it. None have succeeded. Most have actually exploded."

"Explo . . . plo . . . ploded?" said Gormy, his blue lips quivering.

"Did I not mention that before? Oh yes, Rock-throwing is a very explosion-heavy pastime. It's one of the few things that can make a monster pop without the slightest warning.

Even an expert rock-thrower must be on his guard. A careless lift here, a sloppy lob there, and **boom!** No more monster."

"Can . . . can you throw the DO NOT THROW rock?" stuttered Gormy.

"What, and risk exploding all over the flower beds? Your mother would kill me! No, I've realized this rock simply *cannot* be thrown. That's why I carved DO NOT THROW on to its face."

"I bet *I* can throw it!" said Gormy confidently. This time Grumbor did not laugh.

"I said *no*," he said sternly. "It's too dangerous, and you're much too young to be exploding. That rock *cannot* be thrown. And unless you want to be sent to your room for a hundred years, you'll leave it well alone. Do I make myself clear?"

"Yes, Dad," said Gormy quietly.

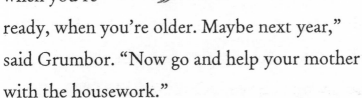

"We'll come back to throwing when you're ready, when you're older. Maybe next year," said Grumbor. "Now go and help your mother with the housework."

Next year? Gormy thought. *Housework?*

This was turning out to be the worst day *ever*.

3
Throwing the Unthrowable

That night, Gormy lay awake in bed. An idea was forming in his brain. The idea had just started turning into a plan when Mike scuttied in through his window.

"Still thinking about the DO NOT THROW rock?" said Mike.

"How did you know?" asked Gormy.

"Oh, I know that *thinking-about-doing-*

something-you-shouldn't-think-about-doing
look. You get it almost every day."

"Well, *this* time it'll be worth it," said Gormy.

Gormy waited until his parents had gone to sleep, then he and Mike sneaked downstairs. They crept out of the back door and down the garden. There, in the moonlight, was the DO NOT THROW rock.

"I don't know about this, Gormy," said Mike. "You don't want to explode. Or even worse, get in trouble with your dad."

But Gormy wasn't listening. He grasped the rock at the base with both paws. It was five times bigger than he was and eleventeen times as heavy.

Gormy held his breath and lifted with all his might. His blue face went purple and his fur stood on end. His whole body began to shake, and steam shot out of his ears. A sound came from his nose which sounded exactly like fifty pigs falling off a cliff.

He started sweating green smoke, then made a noise, which was the very first of its kind:

"GaNNNaBhUrNababaF eeeTPuPTooOOOOGN!"

"Blimey!" said Mike. "You're doing it!"

As slowly as the workings of a sheep's brain,

Gormy lifted the unthrowable rock above his head. By now, Gormy was fairly convinced that he was going to explode any second. But what a way to go! He summoned every last ounce of his strength, and threw!

Thod

"Blimey! you did it!" said Mike.

"I did it!" repeated Gormy. A new-found sense of monstrousness filled him to the brim. He hadn't thrown the rock very far, but he hadn't exploded either! He grabbed Mike and hugged him in delight. He didn't even mind how slimy and pooey Mike was!

It was a few moments later that Gormy noticed a small, dark blob where the DO NOT

THROW rock used to stand. It was very much like any other small, dark blob, and really not much to look at.

That is, until it started to *move*.

4

The Thing Under
the Rock

Gormy and Mike stared as the dark blob began
to uncurl. A long spindly arm appeared, then
another! Shortly after that a leg appeared. The
shape unfolded and unfurled until, finally, it had
a head, two arms and two legs.

It was an odd-looking something-or-other,
even by monstrous standards. It was a little
smaller than Gormy, with a round body and

long, thin limbs. Its skin was smooth and shiny and it had a round head, and gleaming, beady eyes.

"What is it?" whispered Gormy.

"Dunno," replied Mike.

"Bless my bones! What a relief!
I was mashed under there
like some tenderized beef.
My legs are all crunchy,
my arms are all dangled!
And look here at this,
my nose has been mangled!"

The something-or-other rubbed its nose back into shape, before fixing its gaze on a puzzled Gormy.

"Um, hello," said Gormy. "My name's Gormy Ru—"

"The question to ask is:
what is my name?
One day to the next, it is never the same!

In the east, I'm Old Nucksy,
or 'Nucks' if you wish,
but west of the glen
I'm the Black Stony Fish.
Where there's sea and there's sand,
call me Tricksy-to-Tell.
But I'll give you a secret,
since you've treated me well."

"What's he on about?" asked
Mike.

"What secret?" said
Gormy, trying to keep up.
The something-or-other
jumped up and down in
excitement.

"My secret name!
It's the point of this rhyme,
so keep it remembered
and keep it in mind!
For if you forget it,
I'll never be seen,
but you'll know I'm around
by the trouble there's been."

"Blimey, he goes on a bit, doesn't he?" said
Mike.

"So without more ado
(and so you don't make a fuss)
I present you my name,
it's **THE IKUM FLOOKUS!**"

Then for no reason at all, the something-or-other started to giggle. It giggled and giggled and giggled, and as it giggled, it started to fade. Within moments, it had vanished into thin air!

"That's a nice trick," said Mike. "He could use that at parties."

"What was that all about?" said Gormy.

"Beats me," said Mike. "I tell you what though – throwing that unthrowable rock makes you at least twice as monstrous as any monster I've ever seen!"

Gormy swelled with pride. Even though he could never tell his father that he'd disobeyed him (for fear of being sent to his room *for ever*) he was delighted to be the Most Monstrous Monster (Probably in the World) Ever!

Gormy said goodnight to Mike and crept back into the house. It wasn't until he was climbing into bed that he heard something behind him. He turned around to see his bedroom door swinging on its hinges, but there was nothing there.

Just the faint sound of giggling. . .

Morning Mischief

When Gormy awoke the next day, he had all but forgotten about the giggling something-or-other. Anyway, he was so excited about how monstrous he had become that nothing else seemed to matter.

Gormy trekked excitedly across the bathroom (which, like all the rooms in the house, was monstrously big) and began the long climb up to the sink. At the top he began his usual routine of fur washing and fang brushing.

Now you might think that being clean and being monstrous are two very different things, but as Gormy's father always said, "The key to monstering is to know *why* you're monstrous. If you smell bad, how will you know whether it is you, or your smell, that is terrifying?"

Gormy had just squeezed some fangpaste on to his brush when he heard a giggling sound behind him. He looked round just in time to see the door open and close all on its own! He would have thought more about it, but as he put the fangbrush into his mouth. . .

"BLeUrgh!"

said Gormy. It wasn't fangpaste at all!

Fangpaste (as anyone with a passing
knowledge of monsters will tell you) is black
with green stripes and tastes like sweaty armpits.
This was all blue and minty-tasting! It was the
most horrible thing Gormy had ever tasted, and
he had to try very hard not to be sick.

In an attempt to wash away the freakishly
fresh taste, Gormy turned on the tap and took a
few gulps of water. After spitting into the sink,

he turned off the tap. Or at least, he tried to.

He turned and turned and turned, but the tap wouldn't turn off. In fact, the more he turned, the more water seemed to

FoOOoOooOSH

out. Gormy turned and turned and turned until... **tunk!**

The tap came off in his hands!

Gormy hung on to what was left of the tap as the water flowed more and more quickly into the sink. It poured over the rim and

KoSOOOShed

on to the floor.

It'll fill the whole bathroom! thought Gormy. He decided this was one of those extremely rare moments when he really should get his parents.

He tried scrambling down from the sink but the water carried him over the edge. He landed on the floor with a **SPOSH!**

By now the water was spilling over the sink like an enormous waterfall. It began to fill the bathroom. Within moments the water rose from Gormy's knees to his chin. He banged on the door.

"Mum! Dad!" he cried. It was the last thing he said before the water lifted him off his feet. He was flung, weightless, around the room. Soon the whole room would be filled and he would be under water!

Gormy was just starting to get a bit worried

when he spotted the door handle. There was only one thing for it – Gormy took a deep breath into all of his four lungs (and a small one into his spare lung) and dived under. He swam as hard as he could towards the handle.

He had to dodge a bar of soap and his father's favourite rubber duck, but before long he made it! He grabbed the handle and turned with all his might.

After a few (very long) seconds, Gormy felt the giant bathroom handle turn. The door swung open with an almighty

SPOOOOOOOOSSSSH!

The great tidal wave of water cascaded out of the bathroom and down the stairs!

bump

POOsh

Slish

bump

bu-dump

ga-damp

114

Gormy was carried helplessly down the stairs (along with most of the contents of the bathroom!) and all the way to the bottom, through the hall and into the kitchen, before skidding to a halt at his mother's feet.

"Gormy Ruckles, what on Peatree Hill have you done?"

"N-not me!" gasped Gormy, dragging himself to his feet. "The t-tap. . ."

"Are you trying to drown us all?" asked

Gormy's mother. Gormy was about to protest his innocence when he heard *that* sound again. That *giggling* sound. He looked around to see the kitchen door open and swing shut ... all on its own!

"Did you see that?" he said.

"Don't interrupt!" screeched Gormy's mother. "Honestly, Gormy, sometimes I wonder what goes on in that little blue head of yours. Look at this mess! Well, if you've time enough to get into mischief, you've time enough to clean all this up."

"But it wasn't —" began Gormy.

"And when you're finished with *that*, you can do the washing up!" continued his mother.

"And when you're done with that you can help me paint the shed," said Grumbor, strolling into the hall. "Looks like you've got a busy day ahead. . ."

"But . . . but. . ." Gormy began.

"But me no buts, I'll have no buts butted about," said Gormy's mother. "I need everything to be perfect tonight. We have the Boggles family coming for dinner."

Not the Boggles! Anyone but the Boggles! thought Gormy.

The Boggles were a family of monsters from the next valley. Mrs Boggles was big and boring and *never* stopped talking. She especially liked to talk about her son, Poggy.

Poggy Boggles thought he was the most monstrous monster boy in the whole world. He had a proper roar, could scare six different types of livestock and had two, yes two, long, sharp fangs. Even if Poggy had been the nicest monster boy in the valley (which he wasn't) Gormy would have disliked him intensely.

"Smelly-face Poggy," mumbled Gormy, even though he knew Poggy's face didn't smell of anything much.

"So we'll have none of this nonsense," said Gormy's mother. "I want you on your best behaviour. If in doubt, just copy Poggy Boggles.

 I *don't* want you showing me up, not when Poggy is so *monstrously* well behaved.

You see, he knows the difference between monstrousness and mischievousness. So?

What do you want? Do you want to be monstrous . . . or mischievous?"

"Monstrous," replied Gormy quietly. In fact, he had never felt *less* monstrous in his whole life.

Seventy-seven Saucepans

Gormy had been washing up monstrously dirty saucepans for most of the day. As he polished the seventy-seventh of them to a impressive sheen, he felt rather proud of himself. Each pan gleamed only slightly less brightly than Vongur the Blaze, whose head was an actual sun.

Gormy stepped back to admire his gloriously horrible reflection in one of the pans. He was baring his one quite good fang when (for the third time that morning) he heard the strange giggling sound. He spun around to see the kitchen door swing on its hinges.

There it is again! he thought. *The giggling something-or-other from last night! What was it called? The Ookum Fleekus? No, that's not it...*

Gormy put the giggling something-or-other's name to the back of his mind for the moment. He pinned back his pointy, blue ears, and followed the giggling sound upstairs.

"I can hear you!" said Gormy. He searched his room, his parents' bedroom, the spare room and even the room of doom and gloom (which, it turned out, was just a big cupboard) but there was no sign of anyone. *Where can it be?* thought Gormy. He was about to give up when he heard a sound so deafening that the whole of Peatree Hill jumped into the air.

Goooorrrrmmmy!!!

Gormy raced downstairs to the kitchen! He was met at the door by his mother, looking even more angry than the time he'd accidentally eaten her pet squirrel.

"What in the name of the Seven Signs of Monstering do you call this?"

Gormy peered around the kitchen door. He immediately wondered how long he'd been upstairs. The saucepans were covered in paint!

All seventy-seven had been daubed, splashed and dunked in a bright combination of blues, pinks and yellows (the colours of a monstrous shed!). Not only that, but the whole kitchen was covered. The walls dripped with paint, plipping and plopping into bright pools on the floor. Even the air was thick with a painty fog, which settled like multicoloured dew on Gormy's fur.

"I . . . I didn't . . . I . . . I cleaned. . ." began Gormy, his eyes wide with disbelief.

"You call this **CLEANING?**" bellowed Gormy's mother, her words sparking like lightning in the air. "Is this your idea of a joke? Well, I'll tell you what, there's a time and a place for jokes, and it's at four-fourteen on the fifth of Febtember at the Festival of Foolery and Flim-Flam! It's NOT when we're about to have the Boggles over for dinner! What were you thinking?"

"But it wasn't me! I polished—" began Gormy.

"This is exactly the sort of behaviour I was talking about!" interrupted Gormy's mother. "I can't imagine Poggy making mischief, can you? I can't imagine Mr and Mrs Boggles having to tell

Poggy not to splash paint all over the kitchen!"

By now, Gormy's mother was shouting so loudly that Gormy almost didn't hear the sound of giggling.

I knew it! thought Gormy. *It's the Ookum Fleekus . . . the giggling something-or-other! It's trying to get me into trouble!*

He was about to tell his mum all about the DO NOT THROW rock and the giggling something-or-other when he heard his father's voice.

"Who's used up all my paint?" said Grumbor, coming into the kitchen from the garden. He was holding the one remaining tin of bluey-pinky-yellow paint.

"Um . . . it was . . . the . . . uh. . ." Gormy stuttered. He knew he couldn't tell his father about the giggling something-or-other without revealing where it had come from, and that would mean being sent to his room for a hundred years. That was a long time – even for a monster. Gormy bit his lip and said nothing.

"At least have the good manners to admit to what you've done! Go to your room!" screamed Gormy's mother, the hairs on the back of her neck (all three thousand and eight of them) standing angrily on end. She carried on screaming so loudly that Gormy didn't even hear the sound of giggling which followed him up the stairs. . .

A Sticky Situation

Gormy made his way to his room and angrily kicked open the door. He lazily pushed the door closed. His hand immediately stuck to it. He tried to pull it away, but it was glued fast! Gormy sighed a long sigh and slumped to the floor, his hand still thoroughly stuck.

"What's all this then?" said Mike as he scuttied in through Gormy's window.

"What does it look like? I'm *glued* to the door," said Gormy impatiently. "Do you remember that thing under the DO NOT THROW rock?"

"The Ookum Fleekus?" said Mike. "No, wait, that's not it. . ."

"Well, *whatever* its name is – it's been playing tricks on me all day, and I've been getting the blame. I know it's here somewhere because I can hear it giggling. But I just can't find it."

"Oh, I know that feeling. I spent a

whole day following a nice smell of dung but never found it. I did find two twigs and a penny, but when you want dung, only dung will do," said Mike. He stroked his chin thoughtfully. "What we need is to plan out some sort of a plan. A plantastic, plantabulous plan to catch that Ookum Fleekus . . . Eekum Flaykus . . . giggling something-or-other and put it back where it came from."

"Yeah, right back under that stupid rock! Splat!"

The next moment, Gormy's mother burst into Gormy's room, slamming the door (and poor, stuck Gormy) hard into the wall.

"Gormy? I want you downstairs now! Gormy? Where are you?" she barked.

"Here I ab, Mub," said Gormy, holding his

squashed nose. He poked his head round the door.

"What are you doing behind there? Not planning any more *mischief*, I hope," said Gormy's mother. "Now, you listen carefully, Gormy Ruckles, because I'm only going to say this once. I don't know what's got into you, but this dinner party is happening in less than an hour, whether you like it or not. So I'm giving you a choice – you can behave yourself, or you can never see Poggy or any of your monster friends ever again. Do I make myself clear?"

Gormy didn't actually have any other friends, and he certainly didn't like Poggy, so this didn't seem like much of a threat. Still, he decided just to say "Yes, Mum," and leave it at that.

"Good," said Gormy's mother. "Oh, now,

look at the time, the Boggles will be arriving in an hour! I have to check the horse is cooked!"

And with that, Gormy's mother tramped downstairs, talking to herself about the best sauce to serve with horse.

"Well, that's a bit of bad timing," said Mike. "If that Ookum thingy gets up to mischief tonight, I can't see your mum being too happy. "

Gormy squinted his eyes, as if thinking very hard indeed.

"'*Can't see...*' That's it! Mike, you're a genius!"

"About time somebody noticed," said Mike, who then looked a bit confused. "Eh?"

"I've got a plan," said Gormy. "We're going to make the Ookum ... giggling something-or-other easier to see!"

Operation: Catch the Giggling Something or Other (Or: Gormy's Secret Plan)

Sorry, this chapter is secret. You don't want the *you-know-what* finding out about it, do you?

Meet the Boggles

With the plan in place (and after Mike had kindly chewed Gormy's hand free from the door), Gormy made his way downstairs and into the dining room. Laid out on the table was the most tremendously monstrous feast Gormy had ever seen. In order of tastiness, there were:

- **Seven sheep, raw**

- Six hundred and six pounds of lightly smoked cow

- One just-ripe horse, carefully stuffed with fifteen more horses

- Bat soup, made entirely of bats who died from a thorough batting

- Three well-fed donkeys

- Two hundred large pebbles, to aid digestion

- Various choice morsels of hoomum

Gormy jumped as the doorbell rang. Well, roared. Monstrous doorbells roar, wail or sneeze, depending on the season.

"Gormy, get the door!" came his mother's cry. "I'm up to my horns in horse!"

Gormy scrambled and leaped his way to the

handle (monsters' doors are necessarily large) and opened the door. As he landed, he was met by the smug-looking face of Poggy Boggles.

"Hello, Gormy," said Poggy. He always said "Gormy" in the same way, drawn out and sneering, as if the name didn't taste nice.

Poggy was taller than Gormy, with three beady yellow eyes, two tails, and a fairly impressive covering of neat, light-green fur all over his body. Down his back an assortment of small bumps and horns made him look particularly monstrous for his age.

"Aren't you going to grow at all, Gormy? You're just as short as last time," added Poggy.

"Not like Poggy! He's already as tall as a Brog-Mangler and twice as wide," said Mrs Boggles as she swept into the house on her four stumpy legs. She was an impressively hideous monster, with short, clawed hands and a huge green mane of hair running all the way down her back. She leaned down and poked Gormy in the belly with one of her claws. "You're not getting enough protein. Our son Poggy eats a goat a day. Two if he's been out monstering!"

Poggy's been out monstering already? thought Gormy. *But he's the same age as me!*

"Don't prod the boy," said Mr Boggles. He was smaller (and quieter) than Mrs Boggles. His skin was brown and rough like bark, and he had long back legs and a tail. He looked a bit like a cross between a tree and a dinosaur. Gormy thought he was quite nice – even if he was Poggy's dad.

"Evening, Slog! Evening, Volga!" said Gormy's mother as she came into the hall. "How lovely to see you. Why, Volga, you look simply horrendous!"

"Thank you for noticing," said Mrs Boggles. "I've just had my horns done."

"Well, do take your seats at the table. Gormy, why don't you sit next to Poggy?"

Sit next to smelly-face Poggy Boggles? This day can't get any worse! thought Gormy.

But of course, it was going to get a *lot* worse. . .

Bat Soup

As the Ruckles and the Boggles sat down for dinner, Mrs Boggles immediately started talking about Poggy again.

"Poggy's quite the monster-in-the-making," she said, forcing a chunk of horse down her throat. "He can scare, stomp and spit all at the same time. It's quite unheard of for a monster boy of his age. You should see him throw a rock, there's no ear-steam at all."

Gormy longed to tell them all about the DO NOT THROW rock. He put his hand over his mouth to stop the words coming out.

"I've thrown fourteen different things," said Poggy. "I can throw a log without thinking about it. And last week, when I was out monstering all on my own, I threw a baby cow at some hoomums. It was so monstrous. I'm even better at throwing than Father."

"Well, I don't know about that. . ." began Mr Boggles.

"Oh hush, dear, you can barely throw a weasel with your bad back," said Mrs Boggles. "We're hoping to get Poggy a throwing scholarship at one of the better monsterversities," said Mrs Boggles.

"Can you throw, Gormy?" scoffed Poggy, nibbling on a sheep's ear.

By now Gormy was bursting to tell them how monstrous he was!

"He's not quite managed it yet, but it won't be long," said Gormy's mother.

"It's hard to throw anything if you're really,

really small," said Poggy.

Small? I threw the unthrowable rock! thought Gormy. He couldn't keep quiet any longer – he decided he would rather be sent to his room for a hundred years than allow Poggy to gloat for another second.

"Well, *actually*, Poggy, I threw the—" he began.

"Gormy! Fetch another bowl of bat soup," said Grumbor.

"But I was just going to say—" began Gormy.

"*Now*," said Grumbor, not looking up.

"Maybe he's too small to carry it," said Poggy, just loudly enough for everyone to hear.

Gormy sighed, and hopped down from the table. He made his way into the kitchen. There was no sign (or rather, sound) of the giggling something-or-other. He fetched the soup and carried it carefully (the bowl was at least three times his size) into the dining room.

"Bat soup is my absolute favourite!" said Mrs Boggles, drooling all over the table. "Honestly, you should see our Poggy catch bats of an evening; he's as fast as a dragon!"

"Bats are easy," said Poggy. "I can catch two at a time."

And with that Mrs Boggles dug her spoon into the soup.

"Ghaaaaahhhh!"

she screamed as sixty enormous bats flew out! They flapped around her head like a dark cloud, getting trapped in her enormous mane and flitting in and out of her nostrils.

"Shouldn't those bats be battered?" said Mr Boggles as he watched Mrs Boggles trying to pull them out of her nose.

"They *were* when I cooked them," said Gormy's mother, her eyes glowing a furious red.

"Gormy!"

"The bats! They're flying around my brain!" screamed Mrs Boggles. By now, she had both arms all the way up her nose. Mr Boggles tried to pluck the bats out of the air with his long tongue, but he ended up wrapping it around Mrs Boggles' face.

Gormy's mother tried in vain to untangle them, all the time shouting, "GORMY! Come here this instant!"

But Gormy wasn't listening to his mother. Instead he closed his eyes, pinned back his pointy blue ears and waited for the giggling to start.

It was time to put his plan into action.

Follow the Footprints

The giggling something-or-other's giggle was unmistakable. It was here! Amid the chaos of the bats and the entangled monsters, Gormy turned to see the kitchen door swing on its hinges.

"Mike! Now!" cried Gormy. On the other side of the kitchen door, the little scuttybug pushed hard against the last tin of bluey-pinky-yellow paint. He knocked it over and

SpLoOOOOrrrP

spilled the paint all over the floor.

Immediately three footprints appeared in the paint!

SPLOT

SPLAT

SPLUT

Gormy raced into the kitchen, just in time to see a trail of painty footprints leading out of the kitchen and into the hall.

"Mike! Execute Operation Catch the Ookum ... whatever! Go to Stage Two! Stage Two!" yelled Gormy as he raced after the footprints!

"Gormy Ruckles, you get back here this INSTANT!" screamed Gormy's mother.

Gormy chased after the footprints through the hall, into the study and out into the monstering room. Two seconds later he was met by the sneering face of Poggy Boggles.

"You're in so much trouble, Gormy."

"Get out of the way! I've got to follow those footsteps!" said Gormy.

"It's no good making excuses, I've caught you

and I'm *telling*. Run away if you like. I'll follow you and tell everyone where you are," said Poggy.

"Fine," said Gormy. "Try and keep up." Gormy pushed past Poggy, who chased after him, saying things like "I'm so telling!" and "You'll never go to monsterversity at this rate!"

They raced through the hall, out of the monstering room, into the pantry, through the cellar (picking up a much-needed goat-biscuit on the way – chasing is hungry work), up the stairs, out of the bathroom, through his bedroom, past the room of doom and gloom, out of the window. . .

And on to the roof! The footprints stopped at the edge, before the long drop to the garden below.

"You're trapped, there's nowhere to run!" said Gormy. "You may as well show yourself, I know you're here!"

"Who are you talking to?" said Poggy.

"The giggling something-or-other! The Ookum Fleekus . . . oh, *whatever* it's name is!" said Gormy. Then a strange thing happened. He saw the expression on Poggy's face change. It went from its normal sour smugness, to something entirely more *horrified*.

"Not . . . you don't mean . . . not . . . the *Ikum Flookus*?" whimpered Poggy.

And with that, the Ikum Flookus appeared!

"AaaAAAaaaHH! Not again! Mother! Save me!" squealed Poggy, and ran as fast as he could in the other direction. In fact, he entirely forgot he was on the roof. He kept running into thin air and plummeted with an

AAAAAAAAHHh KLUD!

to the ground below.

"That's it!" cried Gormy. "Ikum Flookus! Your name is Ikum Flookus!"

The Ikum Flookus disappeared, then immediately reappeared. It was then that Gormy realized something very important indeed.

The name! The name made him appear and disappear!

It was too tempting not to try again.

"Ikum Flookus!" cried Gormy, and the Ikum Flookus disappeared again. "Ikum Flookus! Ikum Flookus! Ikum Flookus!" he shouted, and the Ikum Flookus disappeared and reappeared over and over.

"Stop it, you gob-rot!
I'm not playing this game,
But I'll be back to torment you,
and with a new secret name!"

The Ikum Flookus leaped off the roof! It bounced like a rubber ball on the ground and started running down the garden.

"Gormy!" came a cry. It was Mike the scuttybug! He had clambered on to the roof, dragging the enormous, empty paint tin behind him. He let the tin go, and it rolled down the roof. "Grab it!"

Gormy skidded down the roof towards the tin, snatching it by the handle. He steadied himself on the edge of the roof, mustered all of his monstrous might, and threw!

Fwweeeeeeeeee

The tin flew through the air! For a moment it seemed as if it would fly for ever. Then, slowly, it began to fall towards the ground. Down and down it fell, gathering speed until,

klump

The tin landed right on top of the Ikum Flookus!

"Now *that* is throwing," said Mike.

12
One More Throw Before Bedtime

Gormy clambered back into the house, and out into the garden.

"GORMY!" cried his mother. "I see you! You come here right NOW!"

Gormy sped down the garden, hotly pursued by his mother and the Boggles. In the distance, he could see the Ikum Flookus trying to escape from under the tin, which rattled and shook. He had almost reached the tin when his mother grabbed him by the ear.

"Gormy Simpsumptitude Ruckles!" said his mother, using his incredibly embarrassing middle name (all monsters are traditionally cursed with a horrible middle name. They're considered a good way of keeping even the most monstrous monster humble). "You are in *so* much trouble! I warned you! Go to your room this instant, and don't think about coming out for a hundred, no, a *thousand* years!"

"Actually, I think he's done rather well," came a voice so thunderous that it almost started to rain. Gormy's father emerged from the shed, one of his vast arms held behind his back. "You see that tin? Under that tin is an Ikum Flookus."

"What?" cried Mrs Boggles. "An *actual* Ikum Flookus?!?"

"Oh yes, an actual Ikum Flookus," repeated Grumbor with a smile. "The *same* Ikum Flookus that your son Poggy let loose in *your* house last week. The same Ikum Flookus that you begged *me* to catch because none of you could. Not even after a whole month of mischief. . ."

Poggy ran into his mother's arms. He had clearly been squashed by the fall – he was now slightly shorter than Gormy.

"Mummy! Daddy! Save me! The Ikum Flookus is after me!" he sobbed.

"No harm done," said Grumbor. He turned to Gormy. "You see, Gormy, the key to monstering is knowing when to trust in your own monstrousness. And if that means ignoring *everything* that your parents tell you, so be it. You're the first monster boy to trap an Ikum Flookus all by himself since ... well, since *I* was a monster boy."

"Oh, Grumbor, honestly!" said Gormy's mother, trying to sound disapproving. But she was so pleased that Gormy had been more monstrous than Poggy Boggles that (would you believe it?) she started to giggle.

"Shall we put things back as they should be?" Grumbor said to Gormy. He brought his mighty hand from behind his back. He was holding the DO NOT THROW rock. "I've

been keeping this safe for you, Gormy.
I thought you might like one more throw before
bedtime. "

Grumbor handed the DO NOT THROW
rock to Gormy, who tried not to show how
heavy it was. He summoned every last ounce of
strength, and threw!

The rock landed on the tin, squashing it flat
and trapping the Ikum Flookus underneath.
Gormy and his father looked at each other and
smiled, while Gormy's mother shot a smug look
at Mr and Mrs Boggles.

"Staying for pudding?" she asked, with a
broad smile.

"Um, no, we'd better
not," said Mrs Boggles.
"Poggy's not very well."

"Save me, Mummy,
don't let it get me. . ."
squeaked Poggy, in a
voice as tiny as a
scuttybug's.

"Shame," said
Grumbor.

"See you soon. If you have any other problems with *ikum flookuses*, do let us know. I'm sure Gormy can sort it out for you."

In that moment, even Gormy started to giggle.

Lesson six hundred and threety-three: How to Catch an Ikum Flookus

As he helped his parents clean up the painty footprints, Gormy could hardly believe it had all just been another lesson. It turned out the DO NOT THROW rock was just a rock. It wasn't unthrowable at all. His father had just pretended it was. He knew Gormy would want to throw it and that he would accidentally release an Ikum Flookus.

You see, an Ikum Flookus is just about the most mischievous, trick-playing, trouble-making creature in the world. Trapping one (even if you released one in the first place) is even more monstrous than rock-throwing.

That night, before he went to bed, Gormy opened his **How to be a Better Monster** book at a blank page. He wasn't sure what to write down. He stared out of his window, down the garden towards where the DO NOT THROW rock lay. Then he remembered what his father had said, about trusting in his own monstrousness.

"I suppose the only thing more monstrous than catching an Ikum Flookus," said Gormy with a more-than-slightly monstrous grin, "is catching one all over again. . ."

MONSTER TROUBLE

A Day Like Any Other

Gormy's day started much like any other. He woke up thinking about monstering (after a whole night dreaming about monstering), and decided that today was the day that he was going to become the most monstrous monster ever.

He jumped out of bed, stretched his tail and straightened his pointy blue ears. Then he measured his one, quite good fang with a piece

of string to check whether it
had grown (it hadn't).

Gormy scampered
downstairs, eventually
arriving at the bottom

(monstrous stairs are tremendously long) to the

SpOrP!
GLOtch!
SpoOOoorp

of his mother mincing a cow for cow jam.

Gormy's mother, Mogra, was a monster of the
hairy, pink variety. She was ten times hairier and

pinker than any animal you could imagine and was so big that Gormy could hide between her toes.

"I hope you're hungry, Gormy – the jam's almost ready," said Mogra.

Gormy licked his lips in delight (being careful not to cut himself on his fang). As he clambered eagerly up an enormous chair leg to the table, he noticed his father by the window.

Grumbor was even bigger than Mogra, and had so many horns and tusks that hugging him was actually dangerous. He was staring intently into the garden.

"What are you looking at, Dad?" said Gormy.

"There's something out here that I think you should see," said Grumbor in a voice so rumbling that it made the jam curdle.

"What is it?" said Gormy. Grumbor's huge hand swept down and scooped Gormy up to the window. Gormy looked out.

"Snow!" he cried in astonishment.

Sure enough, the whole garden was covered in a thick layer of bright, white snow. It was everywhere, from the lawn to the top of the hedges, to the tip of the Very Tall Tree. Even Gormy's treehouse, which nestled in the Very Tall Tree's highest branches, was covered.

"Lovely, isn't it? We haven't had snow in Octobuary for years," said Gormy's mother, dipping one of her massive claws into the jam and tasting it. "Needs more cow," she added to herself.

"Can we go outside and play?" asked Gormy, beside himself with excitement.

"Play?" laughed his father, raising two of his eyebrows. "Why would you want to play when you can *monster*? After breakfast, I want you to fetch your **How to be a Better Monster** book, then meet me in the garden for Lesson Six Hundred and Fivety-Seven: Know Your Snow."

A lesson about snow? thought Gormy. *What does snow have to do with monstering?* Never had two more exciting things gone together! Well, not since he tried eating donkey and horse at the same time.

Gormy swallowed his breakfast without

chewing, and after four or five appreciative
burps, he rushed into his bedroom to get his
How to be a Better Monster book.

Know Your Snow

Gormy opened his Big Chest of Monstrously Excellent Things. He rummaged past a fishing rock, a pack of trouble-gum and two bags of boom-balloons, before taking out his **How to be a Better Monster** book. He hurried downstairs into the kitchen, and opened the back door. He was met with a noseful of biting cold air.

"Finally! I thought you'd never open the

door!" said a small, gruff voice. Gormy looked down to see Mike the scuttybug, shivering on the doorstep.

Mike was about as horrid as monstrous beetles get. He ticked every box when it came to ugliness, sliminess and ugly-related sliminess. But he was Gormy's only real friend, and if you ignored the smell, he was really quite nice.

"Mike! Are you all right?" said Gormy, dusting the snow off Mike's back with a furry finger.

"Of course I'm not all right! It's freezing out here!" grumbled the scuttybug.

"Do you want to come inside? I think my dad's just been to the toilet. . ."

"Fresh dung! Great! That'll warm me up," said Mike, happily scuttying inside.

Gormy made his way into the garden. He looked for his father, but he was nowhere to be seen. He thought about waiting patiently, but not for very long. The sight of all that unspoiled snow was just too tempting to resist – Gormy leapt straight in!

FWUMP!

It was even thicker than Gormy had imagined! He was almost up to his belly buttons in it (all three of them!). The freezing snow clung to his fur and sent shivers down his tail. He leapt into

the air again, bouncing around like a happy
Hop-gobbin.

PwOmp! FOmp! PwUmp!

It was then
he noticed a
large, round
mound of
snow. It looked
perfect for jumping into!
Gormy bounded towards it. He took a deep,
cold breath, and leapt!

GReEoOAArgghH!

The mound exploded! Gormy's father appeared, roaring and looking like he was about to swallow Gormy whole.

Gormy screamed and bounced off his father's nose. He landed with a **FLOMP!** in the snow. He was still shaking when Grumbor reached into the snow and pulled him out.

"The key to winter monstering," said Grumbor, as he put Gormy back on his feet, "is to know your snow."

Gormy looked at the place where Grumbor had appeared from. There was a massive, Grumbor-sized hole in the ground. He had dug a hiding place and covered himself with snow . . . just to scare the fur off Gormy!

"Snow may seem like a lot of fun, but for a monster it can mean the difference between scaring and being scared. Knowing your snow will make you a better monster."

"A better monster," echoed an excited Gormy.

"Good. Now look behind you. What do you see?" said Grumbor.

Gormy looked back. It wasn't a difficult question to answer. Even the house was covered.

"Snow?" he answered.

"Here, in the snow – your *tracks*. Anyone can tell where you have been. That is why monsters have tails – to brush the snow behind us, so that no one can tell where we've gone or where we're going. That is how I was able to surprise you. That is how you will become a monster. Not like hoomums. All they do with snow is play in it and throw snowballs and build snowhoomums. It isn't monstrous at all."

Actually, that sounds like quite a lot of fun, thought Gormy, but he decided not to say anything. The next moment, his mother appeared at the back door.

"That's enough monstering for today! The monstersitter will be here any minute," she called. Gormy's pointy blue ears pricked up in horror.

"Monstersitter? Why is a monstersitter coming?" he said, panicking. Being monstersat (which is like being babysat but less predictable) was terribly unmonstrous. In fact, it was only slightly less unmonstrous than the  three most unmonstrous things of all – talking to a hoomum, being a vegetarian, and (worst of all) having a nightmare!

"Great gobs! I completely forgot!" said Grumbor, slapping a huge, clawed hand against his forehead. "Our monsterversary!"

"Monsterversary? What's a monsterversary?" said Gormy.

"Our wedding monsterversary! Tomorrow, your mother and I will have been married for fivety-two and nine-ninetieths! We're going away for the night, so we got you a monstersitter," said Grumbor, tramping back to the house.

"I don't need a monstersitter!" protested Gormy, but his cries were drowned out by the

Krunch!
Grunch!

of his father's footsteps.

Gormy's day had just gone from brilliantly
monstrous to about as bad as bad days get.

Nana the noog

Gormy tramped sulkily back to the house. He had barely had time to brush the snow off his fur when the doorbell sneezed.

"There's the monstersitter now! Be a good little puffball and answer the door," called Gormy's mother from upstairs.

Gormy dragged his feet all the way to the front door, wondering which of the monstersitters it would be. Not surprisingly, it was hard to find anyone to even go near a house full of monsters. Even other monsters were worried Grumbor would stomp on them just for the sake of it. This meant that the monstersitters that did venture to Peatree Hill were particularly strange. They included:

DRUMP THE DUMP –

a perfectly pleasant ogre from the next valley. Drump the Dump smelled so unspeakably dreadful that it made Gormy vomit every time he came near. The house reeked of Drump and monster sick for months afterwards.

YELLOWSOCKS – a tree-gnome with an annoyingly long beard. The main trouble with Yellowsocks was that he was allergic to monsters. He started sneezing the second he saw Gormy, and didn't stop until Grumbor "accidentally" stepped on him.

OLD SPRIGGLE – some sort of cross between a witch and a goblin. Old Spriggle was one of the meanest creatures in the valley. She would only monstersit on the condition that Gormy sang to her constantly.

I bet it'll be someone even worse, thought Gormy. He sighed and opened the door.

A strange creature leapt out in front of Gormy! He screamed for the second time that morning, and jumped so high with fright that his horns hit the ceiling (and monstrous ceilings are very high).

"Got you, didn't I?" said the strange creature. Gormy took a good look at her. She was about as big as a fat hoomum, with huge, bat-like ears and wrinkly, yellowy-green skin. She wore a cloak of rags (that must have been knitted

together in the dark) and had a rather odd
clump of red hair, which sat on her head like a
bad hat.

"I am a noog, but since noogs have no name,
you can call me Nana. And what's your name,
little monster?"

"Gormy Ruckles," said Gormy.

"Noog's alive, what a scary name! You must be
the most monstrously monstrous monster boy

I've ever met! And look at that fang – you could bite off a yobbin's head with that. In fact, you could bite off all four of them!" said Nana the noog.

Gormy was delighted! He had wanted someone to call him monstrous for as long as he could remember (which was precisely as long as he'd had a tail. Monsters can't remember much of anything until their tail grows. Monsters who lose their tails often forget how to be monstrous, and must retrain or take early retirement).

"Such impressive monstrousness deserves a reward," continued Nana the noog. She twirled a fat finger, and in a POP! of colour, a shiny, yellow sweet appeared in her hand. "Here!"

"Thanks!" said Gormy. He took the sweet and popped it eagerly into his mouth. But the moment he swallowed it, **POP!** he turned completely yellow!

"Hee hee! You've been nooged!" laughed Nana.

"How did you do that?" said Gormy, staring in amazement at his yellow paws.

"Just a little old-fashioned magic! It's easy when you know how – and Nana knows best!" said Nana.

Gormy couldn't believe it – real magic!

Things were turning out much better than he had expected!

"Better put you back to normal before your parents notice," said Nana with a wink. Then, with a twirl of her finger,

Gormy was blue again! He tried not to giggle as (one-and-a-half seconds later) Mogra and Grumbor came downstairs.

"It's nice to see you're getting on so well," said Mogra. "You must be the monstersitter?"

"She's a noog, but since noogs have no name, you can call her Nana," said Gormy, suddenly rather excited about being monstersat.

"Well, Nana, I can't thank you enough for agreeing to monstersit. You're the only monstersitter still advertising in the *Monster Gazette*," said Mogra.

"Oh, I love monstersitting – you never know what's going to happen!" said Nana.

"Well, it's time we were off," said Grumbor. "We need to be at the Bog of Horror cave-spa by two o'clock – your mother's having a wasp's nest facial."

Mogra leaned all the way down to Gormy. She opened her huge, pink claw to reveal a small shiny object, tied to a piece of string. She hung it around Gormy's neck. "This is a pinch-bell. If there are any problems, any problems at all, give this a squeeze and we'll come running," she said.

Pinch-bells are sort of like long-distance, monstrous alarms. They come in two halves – one containing the top half of a fairy, the other the bottom. Squeezing the bottom half makes the top half squeal, no matter how far away the halves are. Squeezing the top half isn't recommended, as fairy farts smell surprisingly nasty.

"There's nothing to worry your horns about. I'll take good care of your little monster," said Nana.

Moments later, Gormy watched his parents tramp off into the snow and disappear behind Peatree Hill. Nana the noog closed the door and grinned a wide grin.

"I thought they'd never leave! Let the games begin – race you to the garden!" she cried.

Noog Games

Gormy quickly realized that Nana wasn't at all like his other monstersitters. He'd never known anyone who liked to play as much as she did! They began with a snowball fight – but this was a particularly *noogish* snowball fight. Every time Nana threw a snowball, she twirled her finger and,

POP!

it was transformed! One second it was a snowball and the next it was:

A ROCK
(which hit **Gormy** on the head. As soon as he woke up, he shouted, "That was brilliant!" and immediately made Nana do it again)

A FIREBALL
(which set **Gormy's** tail alight. He was still giggling long after the fire was put out)

A LIVE RABBIT
(which, once caught, served as a delicious mid-game snack)

Next, they set to work building a snowmonster (which was like a snowhoomum but eleventy times more monstrous).

"It's not exactly scary, is it?" said Gormy,
trying his best to fashion claws out of dry twigs.

"I know how we can make it *really*
monstrous," said Nana the noog. Then she
twirled her finger and,

the snowmonster was transformed. It looked
exactly like Gormy!

"It's a snow . . . me!" said Gormy, admiring his
image. Then he turned to Nana and said, "Do you

really think I'm monstrous?"

"Are you kidding? You're *so* monstrous I'm surprised you haven't tried to eat me yet!" said Nana. No one had ever said anything so nice to him!

Gormy swelled with pride. He had completely forgotten why he hated being monstersat. He didn't even mind that his parents had gone to the land beyond the hill without him.
He took the pinch-bell from around his neck and placed it on the snow-Gormy.

"There, now it really looks like me!" he giggled.

For the rest of the day, Gormy and Nana tore around the garden (being careful not to fall in the enormous hole that his father had dug!) playing so many games that you'd need to be a fivety-fingered flummock just to keep count. However, these were no ordinary, monster games like *Stomp on the Village* or *Roar at That!* These were *noog* games, so noogishly noogiful in their noogishness that they were impossible to describe without using the word "noog". Each game was packed with more magic than Gormy could have wished for. By the time the sun slipped behind the Very Tall Tree, Gormy was sure that this was the best day *ever*.

"Noog's alive, aren't you tired yet? You've got more energy than any monster I've ever met! I'm not sure I've got it in me to play Noog-in-the-Middle. . ."

"Noog-in-the-Middle! How do you play that?" asked Gormy, excitedly.

"Right then, first you take three big spoons and an old curtain. Then we do a bit of good, old-fashioned finger-twirling and—"

Nana stopped. She stared into the sky, open-mouthed. The sun had all but disappeared behind the trees, and it was getting dark.

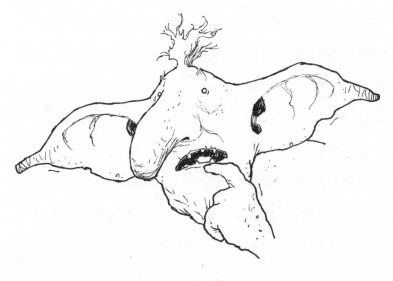

"And then what?" said Gormy, with monstrous anticipation.

"Is it that time already? Noog's alive, where has the day gone? It's time for bed!" Nana rushed back into the house as if her feet were on fire.

"Already? But I don't go to bed until the moon is higher than the Very Tall Tree!" began Gormy, chasing Nana into the kitchen.

"A growing monster needs his sleep. Nana knows best!" said Nana. She hurried Gormy through the hall and all the way upstairs to his

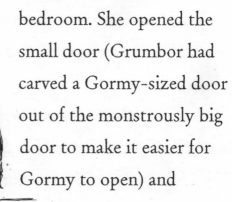 bedroom. She opened the small door (Grumbor had carved a Gormy-sized door out of the monstrously big door to make it easier for Gormy to open) and

nudged him inside.

"Now you must promise me you'll stay in your room until the morning. Don't open this door until the sun rises on the hill, no matter what you hear."

"But—" began Gormy.

"And no sneaking out, mind you. We noogs have terrible eyes but our ears can hear a mouse squeak from one hundred and nine paces. Do you promise?"

"I . . . I promise," sighed Gormy.

"Good boy, and remember, stay in your room! Nana knows best!" said Nana, and shut the door.

What was all that about? We were having so much fun! I knew it couldn't last. . . Ugh, this is why I hate monstersitters, thought Gormy.

He stared out of the window. In the moonlight he could see new snow falling on the ground. Maybe Nana would let him play in it tomorrow, before his parents got back.

Gormy decided it would be best if he went to sleep, even though he didn't want to. He got into bed, pulled the covers over his head and tried counting sheep to help him nod off (of course, monsters count sheep jumping into a boiling pot).

He had reached three hundred and twenty-eight when he finally fell asleep. . .

Stay in Your RoOm

Gormy awoke with a start! What was that noise? It sounded like the house was falling in!

He looked around, but it was pitch dark, so he could hardly see anything (most monsters are rubbish at seeing in the dark, despite mostly monstering at night. At least half the destruction caused by a monstrous rampage is due to them accidentally bumping into things).

KRISH!
KOSH!

The noises were coming from downstairs. Had a pack of wolves got into the house? Gormy wasn't at all keen on wolves. He had managed to scare one once, but a whole pack? That was a different matter. Also, where was Nana? Even with all her magic he wasn't sure she could handle all those teeth and claws.

KRUMP
SMASH!

Gormy remembered his promise to Nana. *Stay in your room . . . no matter what you hear*, she had said. He didn't want to get into trouble. But surely he'd be in more trouble if his monstersitter ended up being mauled to pieces! Plus, curiosity and monster boys go hand-in-claw. Gormy reached for the handle, and opened the door.

KASH!
 KOSH!

Gormy tiptoed on to the landing, and started to creep downstairs. He put his hand against the wall to steady himself and felt something jagged and uneven. Gormy could just make out what it was – *claw marks.* They were much bigger than a wolf could make.

For a split second he thought it might be
something *worse* than wolves. But then, what
was worse than wolves?

CRA-TASH!

Downstairs everything was in pieces. The
carpet was shredded and the old grandmonster
clock lay in pieces on the floor.

The bangs and crashes were coming from the
kitchen. Nervously, Gormy made his way to
the kitchen door and poked his head around.
Something was rummaging around the pantry,
throwing out pots and pans and eating anything
it could.

Whatever it was, it was no wolf. It was

HUGE

and Gormy noticed it had a long, spiked tail, stretching out across the floor.

Gormy stared at it for a moment. Then, for no good reason at all, he said, "Hello?"

The creature in the pantry leapt backwards. It was big as Grumbor – no, bigger! It had dark green scales all over its body and dozens of sharp spikes down its back. It was crouched on all fours, with an extra set of arms thrown in for good measure. Its huge, flat head seemed to be made entirely of teeth and green drool. It also had a rather odd clump of red hair, which sat on its head like a bad hat. It looked, quite frankly, *monstrous*.

"Little monster . . ." snarled the
monster-like creature, in a
voice nineteen times
rougher than
sandpaper.

"Excuse me,
have you seen
Nana?" asked
Gormy in his least
monstrous whimper.

All of a sudden, the monster burped! A drool-
covered ball of dark material flew out of its
mouth and landed

SPLOT!

on the floor. It was Nana's cloak. The monster had swallowed it! Which could only mean one thing. . .

"You ate Nana!" cried Gormy.

"Still . . . hungry . . ." said the monster. As Gormy backed away towards the door, it pounced!

"AAaaaaaaahh!"

screamed Gormy as he leapt out of the way!

The monster crashed into the kitchen door, digging in its claws. It tried to pull away, but it was stuck! It shook frantically to get free. Gormy took the opportunity to do something surprisingly unmonstrous – he ran away as fast as he could!

6

The Room of Doom

Gormy bolted upstairs as he heard the kitchen
door rip off its hinges! He raced down the
landing and straight into the Room of Doom.
Gormy had no idea why it was called the Room
of Doom. It was just a big cupboard filled with
mops and old boxes. Still, he hoped that the big
sign, which read **ROOM OF DOOM** in very
monstrous writing, might be enough to put the

monster off.

What am I going to do?
The monster ate Nana and
now it wants to eat me!
thought Gormy. He'd
never even heard of a
monster-eating monster
before (The Most

Immense Slood liked to *smell* other monsters,
but then he did have forty noses).

Gormy sat huddled by the door listening
to the monster's thunderous footsteps.
With every

– step –

FoOOm!

– the footsteps –

FoOOm!

– got closer!

Then suddenly, they stopped. There was silence. Gormy waited. And waited. In fact, he waited for what seemed like the whole of Mug'Uggin (the secret month, which likes to hide between March and Junetember). After a while he even got a bit bored.

Maybe the monster went home . . . thought Gormy. It seemed pretty unlikely, but (for the second time that night) curiosity got the better of him. He reached for the handle, and opened the door. . .

"BOO!"

The monster was waiting outside the door!
Gormy was now face to face with it, and all he
could see were rows and rows of teeth! He
darted back into the Room of Doom.

"Still. . . hungry. . ." the monster
snarled in a voice that made the
paint on the walls start
to melt. It squeezed
itself into the Room of
Doom and moved
towards Gormy.

"Leave me alone! Aren't you full yet? You just
ate a whole noog!" cried Gormy in desperation.

This made the monster laugh so hard that two of its teeth fell out.

"Stupid little monster . . . haven't you worked it out yet?" laughed the monster, twirling one of its claws. "Nana knows best!"

Gormy's two hearts skipped a beat. Suddenly everything made a horrible sort of sense! Nana telling him to stay in his room, the cloak of rags, the clump of hair! The monster didn't eat Nana . . . the monster *was* Nana!

"Nana?" Gormy whimpered. He barely had time to be shocked by the realization – the Nana-monster opened her jaws, revealing twelve rows of sharp, yellow teeth, and moved in for the kill. Gormy closed his eyes. . .

Just then, Gormy heard a loud, creaking sound. He opened an eye and looked down. He was standing on a large, square platform, which looked slightly different to the rest of the floor. As the Nana-monster lunged, the floor disappeared from beneath him!

It was a trap door!

"AAaaaaaaahh!"

screamed Gormy.

As he fell (and fell and fell!) he realized this might be why it was called the Room of Doom. After all, how many trap doors to who-knows-where are there in your cupboard? He was two-thirds of the way through that thought when. . .

...he hit the floor!

To Pinch the Pinch-Bell

Gormy got to his feet and rubbed his head. A room with a secret trap door – how brilliantly monstrous! High above him, the Nana-monster was trying to squeeze herself through the trap door, but with all of her enormous monstrousness, she was just too big. After a few moments, she gave up and disappeared from sight.

Gormy breathed a sigh of relief. He looked around, but it was so dark he couldn't even see his own nose.

"So, how's that new monstersitter working out? Everything tickety-boo?" said a voice behind him.

"*Mike?* Is that you?" asked Gormy.

"Course it's me! Who else is warming himself up in your cellar?" replied Mike.

"The cellar! So this is where the trap door goes!" said Gormy.

"Yep – although I prefer to use the door – it involves a lot less falling and screaming," said Mike.

"Mike, you've got to help me – it's Nana! The

monstersitter has turned into a monster!"

"A monster, eh? Well, at least now you've got something in common," said Mike.

"But she wants to *eat* me! She's a monster-eating monster!" shouted Gormy.

"Hmm, that could be tricky, what with you being a monster and all. I didn't think monsters ate monsters. Why does she want to eat you?"

"How should I know? I didn't hang around to ask!" said Gormy, looking up at the trap door to see if the Nana-monster had come back.

"Oh well, your mum and dad will be back tomorrow. I'm sure they'll know what to do. You'll just have to stay here where it's nice and warm."

"I can't stay in the cellar until tomorrow night! I'll starve!" cried Gormy (monsters had to eat at least five meals a day to maintain even basic levels of monstrousness).

"Well, you could always give them a bell . . . then again, I'm not sure they'll be too happy about your interrupting their monsterversary," suggested Mike.

"The pinch-bell! I forgot all about it!" said Gormy. He reached for it around his neck, but it wasn't there. "Oh no! I put it on the snow-Gormy! It's in the garden!"

"Then it's lucky for you I know my way around this place. Follow me," said Mike.

Gormy followed Mike's voice through the darkness. They clambered over a crate of digestion rocks and a box of his dad's old monstering magazines, then up some stairs to a large door. Gormy pushed it open and climbed

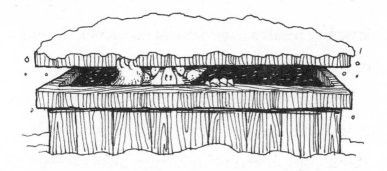

out. He was in the back garden! He could hear
the Nana-monster had returned to the kitchen –
she was loudly smashing or eating whatever she
could lay her claws on.

"Stay quiet! She can hear a mouse squeak from
one hundred and nine paces!" whispered
Gormy. He set about looking for his snowy self,
being especially careful not to fall into the giant
hole his father had dug. Then, in the moonlight,
Gormy spotted something that looked very
much like . . . him!

"There it is!" he whispered. He waded

through the snow until he reached the snow-Gormy. Sure enough there, around its neck, was the pinch-bell. But as he reached out to grab it. . .

Gormy had trodden on a twig!

"I hear you, little monster!" came a cry. Gormy turned back to the house, to see the Nana-monster burst through the kitchen wall!

A shower of bricks, glass, pots, pans and various other monstrous kitchen-related things was sent halfway across the garden! Gormy looked around but there was nowhere to hide! Then he remembered how his father had hidden from him earlier that day. He held his breath, and dived into the thick snow!

"Where are you? I know you're there..." rumbled the Nana-monster, her hot breath melting the snow around her. She squinted in the darkness. She could see Gormy, frozen to the spot with fear. The Nana-monster bared her claws, and leapt!

SPWAT!

Escape to the Treehouse

The Nana-monster landed right on top of
Gormy, squashing him flat! She laughed a deep,
drool-filled laugh, and lifted her foot. But there
was nothing there, only snow! She'd squashed
the snow-Gormy!

"Where are you, little monster?" she bellowed.

Gormy decided, very wisely, *not* to answer.
He couldn't believe his luck! The Nana-monster

had seen the snow-Gormy, and mistaken it for him!

With the Nana-monster still roaring in anger, he dug himself out of his snowy hiding place, and hurried as quietly as he could down the garden. As he moved through the snow, he carefully covered his tracks with his tail, just like his father had taught him.

Gormy quickly reached the Very Tall Tree and started to climb. He didn't look back until he reached the top. Once he was safely in his treehouse, he watched the Nana-monster rampaging around the garden in search of a Gormy-shaped snack.

"That was close! Glad she only ended up stomping the snow-you – it could have been messy otherwise," whispered Mike.

"I still didn't get the pinch-bell," sighed Gormy. "We'll have to stay up here and keep quiet until she goes back in the house."

"Stay here? We'll freeze!" said Mike.

"Shhh! She'll hear us!" whispered Gormy. He looked around for something to help them keep warm. Stuffed into the corner of the treehouse were:

- **ONE HALF-EATEN MOUSECAKE** (which was deliciously rotten but frozen solid)
- **ONE DOG-EARED COPY OF MONSTER BOY'S OWN**

(a popular monster comic featuring tales of daring, adventure and stomping)

- **ONE PILE OF SMALL ROCKS**
  (to throw at passing birds)
- **ONE BLANKET**

The blanket! He'd forgotten he'd left it there! It had been his favourite since he was just a third-and-a-half (his mother had knitted it from his father's summer shedding). He unrolled it and wrapped it around himself and Mike.

Gormy stared out over the land beyond the hill. As the sun began to rise he could see the vast, snowy duvet that covered the fields. It was as if a great frosty winderbeast had thrown up over the whole valley – it was the most beautiful thing he had ever seen. He wondered if he would ever get to monster in it.

"Do you think I'll be a real monster one day?" he whispered to Mike.

"Sure! You'll be the most monstrous monster ever! As long as you don't get eaten by your monstersitter, that is," Mike replied.

Gormy looked back. At the other end of the garden, he could see the Nana-monster, still looking for him. She had ripped up every tree in the garden, and all but destroyed the house.

"At least we're safe here — as long as we stay quiet," said Gormy. He sniffed, and wiped a cold, wet droplet from under his nose. It tickled slightly. He rubbed it again, but it just tickled even more.

"Uh-oh," he said.

"What's the matter?" asked Mike.

"I think I'm going to sn . . . sn . . . sn. . ." began Gormy.

"No, don't!" cried Mike.

"Aa-AA-aaa-cHOOo!"

Treehouse of Terror

Gormy's unfortunately timed sneeze was, in fact, the fourteenth most monstrous sneeze ever heard. It blew all of the snow from the top of the Very Tall Tree, dislodged three pigeons from their perches and scared a sleeping owl to death. And it was more than loud enough to let the Nana-monster know where they were.

"There you are!" she howled, and bounded

towards them! Within seconds, she was climbing the Very Tall Tree!

"She's going to eat me! What are we going to do?" yelped Gormy. He grabbed his pile of bird-pelting rocks, and started throwing them at her. But they just bounced off her scaly skin like they were scuttybug droppings. The Nana-monster laughed, and kept on climbing.

"She's nearly at the top – and there's no way out but down! We're trapped up here! Trust me to be a scuttybug and not a scuttyfly!" cried Mike, scuttying frantically around Gormy's head.

"Fly . . . Mike, that's it! You're a genius!" said

Gormy, suddenly having a monstrous (or monstrously stupid) idea. He grabbed his blanket by all four corners and held it behind him. "Hang on, Mike!"

Gormy ran to the edge of the treehouse. Just as the Nana-monster reached the top, he jumped! He leapt over the Nana-monster's snapping jaws. Mike held on tightly to Gormy's fur as they plummeted downwards. Then,

PWOOOSH!

The blanket opened like a parachute! Gormy was floating through the air!

He soared over the garden, over the hedges, trees and snow-covered lawn. Gormy had never even dreamed of flying (monsters usually dream about roaring, stomping or chomping), but it was monstrously exciting!

If I don't get eaten, I'm definitely going to try this again, he thought. In fact, Gormy was having such a good time that for a second, he forgot all about the Nana-monster.

But only for a second.

"Gormy, she's after us again!" yelled Mike. Gormy turned his head to see the Nana-monster leap out of the tree! She crashed to the ground and immediately started bounding after them and gnashing her jaws. And all the time, Gormy was getting closer to the ground.

"Make us go higher!" shouted Mike.

"I can't! It only goes down!" said Gormy, frantically trying to flap his legs.

"Still hungry!" cried the Nana-monster.

Gormy had almost floated the whole length of the garden. They were almost at the house! As they inched ever closer to the ground, he spotted something glinting in one of the Nana-monster's giant claw-prints.

"The pinch-bell!" he cried. Gormy steered towards it, the snow-crunching sound of the Nana-monster getting ever closer. As they sped towards the ground, Gormy and Mike closed their eyes.

PLOOMP! POMP! KA-FUMP!

Gormy skidded and bounced along the ground like an out of control snowbomb! By the time his brain had stopped rattling, the shadow of the Nana-monster was looming over him.

"Too late, little monster!" roared the Nana-monster and pounced!

GWuMP!

The Nana-monster disappeared into the snow! She was stuck fast in a giant hole – the hiding-hole that Gormy's father had dug the day before!

"The hole . . . she jumped right into it!" said Gormy, as the Nana-monster roared in anger. Gormy didn't waste another second –he grabbed hold of the pinch-bell and squeezed with all his monstrous might!

"I hope your parents heard it," said Mike, shaking the snow off his antennae.

Then a strange thing happened. As the morning sun shone on to the hole in the ground, the Nana-monster stopped roaring. In fact, she went very quiet indeed. Gormy crept towards the hole.

"Where are you going? That's the way to the monster-eating monster!" said Mike.

But what Gormy saw wasn't a monster-eating monster. In fact, it wasn't a monster at all. It was a plain old noog, looking exactly as she had when Gormy first met her.

"Noog's alive, I've done it again, haven't I?"
said Nana.

The Trouble with noogs

By the time Gormy had helped Nana the noog out of the giant hole, she had apologized a total of thirty-eight times.

"This is the trouble with noogs! We're lovely, magical, noogiful creatures by day, and savage, monster-eating monsters by night. It's just one of those things. . ." explained Nana.

"But how come you've managed to be a

monstersitter all this time? You must have eaten every monster boy in the valley," asked Mike.

"All the other little monsters have stayed in their rooms – they've been too tired after a day of noog-games to wake up. And if they do hear me crashing around, they're just too scared to come out. What a brave little monster you must be, Gormy," said Nana.

"I was a little bit scared when you were chasing after me," confessed Gormy, though he tried to sound braver than he felt.

"You won't tell, will you?" begged Nana. "I'd be so lonely without my monstersitting. It's not easy making friends when you turn into a monster-eating monster every night."

image

Gormy couldn't help feeling sorry for Nana. Here he was, trying to be more monstrous, and she wanted to be anything but!

"Don't worry, your secret is safe with us. Right Mike?"

"Naturally! But I reckon we should fix the place up before your parents get back," said Mike.

"My parents! Oh, no! I squeezed the pinch-bell! They'll be on their way back, and the house is a wreck!" cried Gormy, panicking.

"Don't worry, Gormy," said Nana. "I've spent two hundred years cleaning up after myself – all it takes is a little magic. . ."

Actually, it took quite a lot of magic to put the house and garden back the way it was. Nana made her way around the house, twirling her fat finger here, POP! , there, POP! , and everywhere. And with every twirl and POP! something was magically repaired. From the trees, to the walls, to the grandmonster clock – it was all in a day's work for a guilty noog. She even used her magic to close the trap door in the Room of Doom! Before Gormy knew it, everything was back the way it should be.

"Nana, that was amazing!" said Gormy, his mouth agape.

"And just in time – look who's back. . ." said Mike, glancing out of the front window. A second later, Grumbor and Mogra crashed through the door.

"Gormy, my precious furball, where are you?" roared his mother, almost trampling him. "We heard the pinch-bell squeal — are you all right? Was it wolves? How many were there? What happened, Gormy?"

Gormy looked at Nana. For a moment she looked as though she was going to confess all, so he said, "Everything's fine. I, um . . . I had a nightmare. That's it. I had a *nightmare* and I was scared, so I squeezed the pinch-bell," said Gormy, sheepishly.

"You had a *nightmare*?" cried Grumbor, in disbelief. "But monsters don't have nightmares! Monsters are *in* nightmares! You can't have a nightmare, it's . . . it's just not *monstrous*!"

"Oh, leave the boy alone, Grumbor," said Mogra. She grabbed Gormy and hugged him so tightly that he thought he might burst.

When he got his breath back, Gormy breathed an enormous sigh of relief. He hated looking so unmonstrous in front of his father, but he was glad that, for once, no one had got into trouble.

"Well, that's put an end to our monsterversary," grumbled Grumbor, "and I was just about to have my claws buffed. . ."

"You should go back! There's still time! I promise I won't squeeze the pinch-bell again. And Nana's here to look after me, so there won't be any trouble," said Gormy.

"Oh, I don't know . . . are you sure?" said Mogra. "I mean, do you think you could cope with another night of being monstersat?"

"Definitely!" Gormy answered, with a smile.

Lesson six hundred and fivety-seven: Nana Knows Best

After a nice hot cup of sheep tea, Gormy's parents said their goodbyes and set off down Peatree Hill for the second time.

"Thanks for not telling them about the whole noog-monster thing, Gormy," said Nana. "At least now you know *why* you have to stay in your room tonight."

"Don't worry, I've learned my lesson. Nana

knows best!" said Gormy, with a glint in his eye.

"Now you're getting it! Right, then, how about a few noog games to start the day?" said Nana.

"Actually, um, it's been a long night . . . and I'm very tired. I think I might go to bed for the day," said Gormy, yawning a big "look how tired I am!" yawn.

Much to Nana's surprise, Gormy headed straight for his room, yawning loudly all the way. But the second he closed the door, his yawn turned into a grin. It was a grin so full of monstrousness that it actually made Gormy's fang grow a little longer.

Of course, Gormy hadn't learned his lesson at all. He was only going to bed so he'd be wide awake by bedtime! After all, he would much rather give up another day of playing with Nana, so that he could have another night of "playing" with the Nana-monster! It had been the most monstrous night of his whole life!

Gormy wasn't even sure there were enough pages left in his **How to be a Better Monster** book to write down all the monstrous things he'd done – he'd learned how to "know his snow", nearly been eaten *and* stomped on, fallen down a trap door, parachuted out of the treehouse and managed to survive a night with a monster-eating monster! He couldn't wait to do it all over again!

Still, he didn't want to ruin his parents'

monsterversary again. He would have to make it through the night *without* squeezing the pinch-bell. He took it from around his neck, put it into his Big Chest of Monstrously Excellent Things, and locked the chest tight. Then he tucked himself up in bed and waited for it to get dark.

"See you soon, Nana," said Gormy, his grin more monstrous than ever, "and remember – Gormy knows best!"